DATE WITH DEATH.

Books by Elizabeth Linington

DATE WITH DEATH

NO EVIL ANGEL

GREENMASK!

DATE WITH *Death.*

BY *Elizabeth Linington*

HARPER & ROW, PUBLISHERS
NEW YORK

Admire, exult—despise—laugh, weep—for here
There is no matter for all feeling:—Man!
Thou pendulum betwixt a smile and tear.
　　　　　　—BYRON, *Childe Harold's Pilgrimage*

One

_____

IT WAS HALF PAST EIGHT IN THE MORNING OF THE SECOND OF
November. Blessedly, though it was a nice warm sunny day,
the real heat had gone with October, which in southern California it didn't always do.

Lieutenant Eden was on vacation, and nominally the Detective Bureau at the Wilcox Street precinct was in the
charge of the senior sergeant, Ellis. Sergeant Ellis was fussing
and fuming over a vice case—or rather a thing he hoped to
turn into a case by some means; and a new homicide had
turned up overnight. The couple of men on night tour who'd
gone out on that had left notes on it on Maddox's desk. Maddox had, in fact, just come into the office at ten to eight,
read over the notes, and begun to discuss it with Detectives
D'Arcy and César Rodriguez, when the squad-car man called
in about the pig.

The pig was something entirely offbeat, and anyway they
couldn't go question people on that homicide until at least
nine o'clock, so they'd all come up to Higman Avenue in
Maddox's Frazer-Nash, to look at the pig.

Rodriguez was about halfway through _The Reader Is_
Warned, and read a few more pages on the way.

"A pig!" said D'Arcy. "I tell you, Ivor, I used to think Hollywood had kind of settled down. But some of the stuff we've been getting lately—"

They found the address. The squad-car man was waiting for them in the drive: it was a modest little frame house, well kept up, lawn trimmed and neatly tended flower beds near the house. Sounds of altercation came from the back yard. The squad-car man was Stoner.

"It's the *damnedest* thing I ever saw," he said. "What do we do about it, Sergeant? It's round back."

They all walked down the drive, and there was the pig. Inside the fenced back yard. There also were Mr. and Mrs. Clyde Endler, arguing loudly.

The pig was placidly munching on a bunch of asters in full bloom. It was quite a large, well-grown pig, with bulging sides, a sullen expression, and rather malevolent little eyes. Somebody had painted the pig a bright pink all over, and then carefully stenciled blue polka dots all over the pink pig. It was, to say the least, a remarkable sight.

Maddox, D'Arcy, and Rodriguez stared at it and burst out laughing.

"That's right!" said Mrs. Endler bitterly. "Go ahead and laugh! *Cops!* Can't you get it *out* of here? Oh my God, now it's eating my violas!" She turned on her husband. "And you know whose fault it is, don't you? Well?" Mrs. Endler was a little, thin, dark woman, not bad looking; he was a big gangling fellow going a little bald. They were both somewhere in the late thirties.

"Hell, *I* didn't bring the damn thing here, Mae!" he protested. "How the hell should I know who—"

"Mr. Endler just found it here awhile ago when they got

up," said Stoner to Maddox. "I didn't know— I mean, it just looks like a practical joke of some—"

The pink pig moved ponderously away from the flower bed, stood a moment as if in rumination, grunting softly, and then plodded over to the raised bed round a young apricot tree and began sampling the ivy geraniums there. "My God!" said Mrs. Endler passionately. "Look what it's doing. Can't you get it out of here, that's all I—"

Maddox managed to control his mouth and said, "You just—er—found it in the yard like this, sir? When you got up?"

"Yes, yes," said Endler. "How the hell should I know who'd do such a crazy thing? I thought I had the D.T.'s, I saw it, I swear to God!" He mopped his face with a handkerchief. "Well, I mean—a joke's a joke, but—"

"Get it out of here!"

"—the Humane Society," said Stoner *sotto voce*.

Rodriguez looked at the pig and began laughing again.

"*Cops!*" said Mrs. Endler.

The pig grunted and without stopping its sampling of the geraniums began to relieve itself copiously onto the lawn. "My God," said Mrs. Endler, "*look* at it. I just put nine dollars' worth of fertilizer on this grass—"

D'Arcy walked up and inspected the pig closer. "It's a white Poland China, I think," he said.

"How d'you come to know that?" asked Maddox.

"I went to the County Fair once."

"I don't care what *brand* it is," said Mrs. Endler. "I just don't give one damn. All I'm asking is, you should take it away."

Maddox looked at Rodriguez. Rodriguez looked at D'Arcy. The pink pig grunted again and swung around ponderously and started for D'Arcy. D'Arcy retreated hastily. It was a very large pig.

"I thought the Humane Society maybe," offered Stoner.

"By all means," said Maddox. "If we could use your phone, Mrs. Endler?"

"Use it, use it, for God's sake! Just—"

Maddox nodded at Stoner, who started for the house with Endler. "Do you have any idea who might have left the pig here?" he asked the woman. "It was a joke, you think? I don't exactly see—" After all, he thought, a somewhat elaborate and pointless one. He, whoever, had had to get the pig some place, go to a lot of trouble decorating it, and somehow transport it here to the middle of Hollywood—

"Joke, joke!" she said impatiently. "Oh, for the Lord's sake!" The pink pig was now rolling, luxuriously and with sensual hip-swaying motions, in the bed of asters. Mrs. Endler shut her eyes and said, "My God. Oh well, of course you don't know Clyde. It was somebody who *does* know him, that much I can tell you, and I hope you find out *who* because I'm going to sue him for his last cent. *My roses!* I—"

"Oh-oh," said D'Arcy. The pink pig, thoughtfully munching on a rose, evidently had got hold of a thorn. It grunted loudly, spat out the mangled rose and stalk, pawed at its mouth with a front hoof and nearly lost its balance. It swung around again and stared evilly at D'Arcy, who retreated some more.

"I really don't think they're dangerous," said Rodriguez, amused.

"Well, it doesn't look very friendly."

"Why, Mrs. Endler?" asked Maddox. "I don't see—"

"Oh, for *heaven's* sake," she said crossly, "it was somebody who knows how the whole family's been after him about his drinking—heaven knows I've tried every way I can think of—it's all those drunken friends of his down at that tavern, he's never been a real drinker but since he's got in with that bunch, tie one on six nights a week—"

"I do not!" said Endler defensively, coming up in time to hear that. "Well, gee, Mae, not really. I mean, just a few drinks with the guys—"

"Bunch of drunken bums! And I had to put you to bed last night and the night before, didn't I? What do you call *that*, just social drinking like they say?"

"Well, gee, Mae—" Endler had a pleasant, weakly boyish face; he gave her an ingratiating smile. "I didn't *mean*—"

The pig was rolling again. "Some of the pink's coming off," said Rodriguez. "I'll bet it's just that food coloring, something like that." The pig was even odder-looking parti-colored. Maddox stifled another laugh.

As a practical joke—

"Oh, it's just side-splitting, that's what it is!" said Mrs. Endler. "Somebody's real subtle little way of saying you better watch out or you *will* be getting the D.T.'s! I wouldn't put it past your Uncle Henry—he was talking pretty sharp about it to you on Sunday."

"May I have his name and address, Mrs. Endler?" Maddox got out his notebook.

"Why, d'you think it could've been him? Well, I don't know, but— Well, it's Henry Endler, out on DeLongpre. Come to think, though, I don't see how he could have—"

"How did anybody?" asked Endler. "That's a hell of a big pig. God, I've still got a headache."

Indeed, how had anybody? The practical joker must, Maddox thought, have a pickup truck, something like that, because—

Stoner came back. "They said they'd come get it, after I got them to believe I wasn't kidding. I mean, a *pig*."

And such a pig, thought Maddox. And what kind of charge would it be, anyway? Malicious mischief at least, he decided, looking at the havoc the pig had made of Mrs. Endler's carefully tended garden. The pig was now rooting about the lawn; chunks of grass fell under its heedless hooves.

"When are they coming, for the Lord's sake? *Look* at it."

"Well, they said as soon as they could, ma'am."

"Mrs. Endler," said Maddox, stifling another strangled laugh as the pink pig waddled over to the redwood fence and began rubbing against it, shaking the fence dangerously, "could you suggest anyone else who might have—"

"*I* don't know," she said sulkily. "Anybody knows Clyde and how he's got to drinking lately. Listen, you find out who brought that—that *animal* here! *I* don't think it's so damn funny, and I'm going to sue."

"What do you think?" asked D'Arcy. "Malicious mischief, I guess. My God, that pig."

"At least," agreed Maddox, grinning. "But hell, D'Arcy, it might be anybody. How'd we trace him?"

"Where did he get the pig?" asked Rodriguez. "Some lead there, I'd say."

"Oh for God's sake," said Maddox. "We've got this homicide to look at. And something a little funny about that too, ask me." Stopped for a light, he adjusted the rear-view mirror and stared absently at himself in it. Yes, and a party at Dulcie's tomorrow night, and in the middle of a real case (which

the homicide looked like being) he oughtn't to go, damn it—
Because, knowing Dulcie— Well, that whole bit was a mystery he'd never solve, that was all. Why practically every female he met found Ivor Maddox so entirely fascinating—ordinary, under-average-height, thin dark Maddox who was anything but handsome. And of course, same like advice to the young lady getting raped, Relax and enjoy it—if he hadn't been an L.A.P.D. man. This force had some pretty puritanical rules about that sort of thing.

At least, he reflected philosophically, one of the females chasing him wouldn't be around for a while. That poor lush Maggie McNeill. The family had stashed her away in a sanatarium. If they thought she'd be cured they were just fooling themselves, but at least she wouldn't be hanging around Maddox while she was in.

He was thinking about the new homicide when Rodriguez started to laugh again. "That pig! Of all the damn fool practical jokes— A painted pig!"

"The fellow from the Humane Society said it was just vegetable dye," said D'Arcy. "I suppose we ought to have a little look around, try to find out who. No kind of charge, but—"

"Oh, I suppose so."

"This homicide," said Maddox. "Just a little bit more important, hm?"

They agreed to that. Not that most homicides posed any real mystery; in real life, as opposed to the paperbacks, the X responsible for homicide usually showed up rather soon and obviously. The work that had to be done on it was pure drudgery: questioning witnesses, looking through Records, getting statements.

The new homicide that had turned up at one forty-seven

this morning offered, at first glance, plenty of places to look for X and plenty of dull routine legwork to do.

Ronald Morgenstern had been twenty-seven, evidently a bright and ambitious young man; he would have graduated from his law course at L.A.C.C. next June. From the fact that he was going to low-tuition L.A.C.C., which offered numerous night courses, it could be deduced that he had been working his way through school, and that was backed up by the information from Ruth Evans's parents that he'd had a job, he'd worked part time keeping books at a couple of different places. Most of what they had on it, this early, had come from the Evanses last night.

Morgenstern and Ruth had got engaged about six weeks ago. Joe Rowan, who'd done most of the first questioning, said in his notes that the Evanses looked like Money, nothing ostentatious, but solid substantial people—it was an address on Franklin Avenue, which told the story. Not a brashly new exclusive residential section, but an older, old-fashioned street of old-fashioned two-story homes, where Money—of the quiet conservative kind—lived.

Rowan hadn't been able to press the Evanses much, of course, but he'd got what he could, at the hospital. The Evanses had liked young Morgenstern, approved of the engagement. Ronnie and Ruth had intended to be married after his graduation next year. His parents were both dead; his only relatives here were an aunt and uncle, Mr. and Mrs. Goldfarb, who lived in Duarte. He'd had a small bachelor apartment on Ardmore Avenue. Everybody, said the Evanses distractedly, liked Ronnie.

Apparently there'd been somebody who didn't.

Or it could, of course, have been somebody who didn't like

Ruth. You paid your money and you took your choice.

Ronnie and Ruth had gone out on a date last night. He had picked her up at home at seven o'clock, and they'd intended, as far as the Evanses knew, to have dinner somewhere and then go to see the new Disney at Grauman's Chinese Theatre. You could figure some times there, working back from the time the call came in. Dinner, call it an hour, an hour and a half, depending on where they'd gone, if they'd lingered over drinks beforehand—say they got to the theatre for the second running, which would be anywhere from eight forty-five to nine fifteen, and out at around, what, midnight or a bit after. No telling yet whether they'd stopped somewhere for a snack or a drink: no telling how long they'd been parked in the drive of the Evans house on Franklin, before X appeared. Or had X been waiting for them? Evidently.

It was approximately one fifteen when the Evanses, and a number of neighbors, had been awakened by a fusillade of shots. Evans had got up and looked out, had seen nobody moving, but had spotted Morgenstern's car ('56 Chevy two-door, said Rowan's notes tersely) in the drive, with the driver's door open and what looked like a body sprawling half out of the car. He'd gone down in a hurry to investigate, and found both Ronnie and Ruth apparently shot—Ronnie dead, sprawled head first out of the car, and Ruth unconscious and bleeding.

Ruth Evans, when Rowan had left his note, was still alive but in serious condition at the Hollywood Hospital. The surgeon had recovered two slugs from her body which had been dispatched to Ballistics downtown. Morgenstern's body had been sent for autopsy.

A lot of places to go looking, you could say. Some former

9—

boy friend of Ruth's, jealous? Some former girl friend of Ronnie's? That looked likeliest. Question the parents some more, question Ronnie's relatives, his friends, at school, at work. Ask around about Ruth. Had she held a job?

Everybody agreed the shots had been "very loud." A heavy caliber? See what Ballistics said about the slugs.

Maddox sighed. Always plenty to do.

They climbed the creaking stairs of the old precinct house. Maybe someday the city fathers would get around to appropriating enough money to paint the place, at least. And maybe not, too.

In the second office across the hall, as they came by, Sergeant Ellis was leaning across his desk talking earnestly to Sergeant Daisy Hoffman and Policewoman Carstairs. "Listen," he was saying, sounding annoyed, "there's not one goddamn bit of usable evidence on the bastard—the way the damn judges interpret the law—and this new law about resorting— My God, tie both hands behind our backs and expect us to—"

"I suppose Rowan stationed somebody at the hospital," said Rodriguez, "in case the girl comes to and can talk."

"Fisher," said Maddox. "Look, D'Arcy, you chase over there and see the parents again, will you? And, César, let's you and me try to chase down people who knew Morgenstern —at work, at the college."

"Pues sí," said Rodriguez, shrugging. The deadly routine bored him; it was a lot more interesting and complex in print, in the detective novels. He put *The Reader Is Warned* in his jacket pocket. "I'll check the college, O.K.?"

"O.K.," said Maddox. Contact the aunt and uncle, but he hadn't been living with them, would they know much about his friends? Better check where he'd worked first.

— 10

"What about the pig?" asked D'Arcy gloomily. D'Arcy was always gloomy these days. Margaret Talmadge had just got engaged to an American Airlines pilot.

"The pig," said Maddox, "for God's sake. Oh well, I suppose we have to look, where we can. Malicious mischief—" He laughed. "Send out an inquiry to all the hog breeders in the county, have you lost a pig recently. You know, that was a hell of a lot of trouble to go to, just for a silly joke. I wonder—"

The outside phone rang on his desk and he picked it up. "Maddox." Dulcie's party—did he dare go? Knowing just how it would go, her inveigling him to stay on, and damn it, he wasn't any Trappist monk, so the office trying to get him, and— Oh, damn.

"Fisher, sir. I'm at the hospital. We just got the word— Ruth Evans died."

"Oh. So, a double homicide," said Maddox. "Nice. Thanks. Parents there? Of course." Difficult to question the parents, but it had to be done.

"Jealous boy friend," said Rodriguez with a grimace. "Want to bet? Human nature, human nature."

"What we're here to cope with," said Maddox sourly.

That pig . . . Silly damn thing, but have to do a little work at it, he supposed. The homicide came first.

Two

"I JUST CAN'T TAKE IT IN—WHO'D WANT TO—TO HURT RUTH OR Ronnie?" George Evans had said that before, breaking off his answers to Maddox's questions, shaking his head dumbly. "I can't believe anything like this has *happened*, is all. Ruth—"

"I know, Mr. Evans," said Maddox gently. "And I'm sorry to have to bother you at a time like this, but we want to get on it and find out who, you know."

"Yes," said Evans. "Yes." He looked vaguely around the room. "I understand that."

Maddox had waited to see the parents; you couldn't humanely press people at a time like that. He'd talked to the doctor, he'd phoned the surgeon scheduled to do the autopsy downtown; he'd gone through the contents of the girl's handbag, of Morgenstern's pockets. One thing there had been helpful. You wouldn't expect a girl out on a date to have an address book with her, but Ruth had carried a billfold which had everything right together in it, change pocket, bill pocket, about two dozen plastic envelopes for credit cards, license, I.D., and so on, and a small address book at the back; so they had that without questioning the parents.

"Nobody can believe it," said Benjamin Goldfarb. His wife just sat and sobbed. Maddox had come to the Evanses' house half an hour ago to find Evans and the Goldfarbs here; they told him Mrs. Evans was in bed under sedation prescribed by their doctor. He was pleased to find the Goldfarbs here: save a little trip out to Duarte. Goldfarb was a paunchy little dark man with strongly Semitic features; he looked gray and shocked. "It must have been a nut, that's all. Nobody had any reason, either of them—it just doesn't make sense! A nut. My God, Ronnie. I tell you, you had to admire that boy, Sergeant. You really did. A good boy, a fine boy. Ambitious. And after what he'd been through— I dunno if anybody's told you, but he was hurt bad in the same accident where Merla and Joe got killed. His parents. Nearly six years back. He was just in his first year college, he'd had his army service to do, he couldn't go back. Back 'n' forth in the hospital, they had to do some bone grafting and all, and the insurance didn't start to cover it—he was with us then. He worked as he could, but he couldn't go back to school full time until the doctors were finished with him. He was all right again, didn't even limp, they fixed up the leg just fine, you know. And never occurred to him not to go back to college, even if he was older and all. Ronnie was an ambitious boy, Sergeant. A good boy."

The woman just sat and sobbed. "Yes sir, I'm sure he was," said Maddox.

"Why, Mr. Evans here knows that. You both liked Ronnie, didn't you, approved of him, like. Ronnie, he waited a long while before he got nerve, ask Ruth to marry him. He was afraid everybody'd think it was just because—you know—her family's got more money. I'm retired, was in the wholesale grocery business. Joe, he was manager of a Safeway market— But when the Evanses got to know Ronnie—"

"Yes, yes," said Evans tiredly. "But that's what makes all this so incredible. Who could have wanted to— Unless it was just a lunatic."

"Mr. Evans. One thing I want to ask you, about those shots you heard. Were they continuous? Or were there shots, and then an interval, and more shots?"

Evans put a hand to his temple. He was a pleasant-looking man, about fifty; his gray suit was well-cut but he'd dressed in a hurry last night and now his open-collared shirt was rumpled and stained, and he looked very tired. He was, it had transpired, senior partner in a law firm in Hollywood. "I don't remember," he said. "I don't remember at all. I—we were asleep, you know—waking so suddenly—"

"Yes sir." Well, Ballistics would help there. The thing was, though the surgeon had only got two slugs out of Ruth, she'd been shot five times; and the surgeon downtown reported that Morgenstern had been shot four times. That said X must have stopped at some point to reload. Cold-blooded. Offhand, Maddox couldn't think of any gun on the market that would hold that many in one load, barring that Harrington and Richardson nine-shot revolver and that was a .22. It looked as if the gun used had been a heavier caliber.

"Can you think of any former boy friends your daughter may have had, who might have resented her getting engaged?"

Evans looked at him. "I wouldn't think—anything so—"

"You never know how people will act sometimes. Had she dated other young men before she met Morgenstern?"

— 14

"I— Yes, of course. Not—not so many. Ruth's—Ruth was a very serious girl. While she was in college, she went to U.S.C., she was more concerned about her studies. I think it was some time around her junior year she was going some with Frank Gates—he was a nice young fellow too, but I think they were more just—just friends, you know. And then there was Phil Delgado, and a young fellow named—named—Pierce, yes, Bob Pierce—just the casual thing, you know. Ruth was— That's crazy! None of those would—all this time after—"

"Remember any others? Have any idea where those three might be now, Mr. Evans? What work they do?"

"It's crazy," said Evans dully. "She hadn't seen any of them for a long while. Well, last year anyway. When she started going with Ronnie. I don't know where they'd be. They were all in college then—that'd be three, four years ago. Delgado was taking an engineering course. Frank Gates—I think both he and Pierce were in several of Ruth's classes, taking the same course. You do know she was a social worker?"

"No, I didn't, Mr. Evans. One of the things I wanted to ask you, did she have a job?" If so, not of necessity, he thought: not by this house. A lot of thought and money had gone into the decoration here; this was a charming, elegant room, well-designed modern furniture, expensive-looking curtains and carpeting, a light and welcoming room with comfortable chairs.

"Yes. Yes, she worked for the Welfare Board. As a social worker. She was—very much interested in it, and besides she believed—" Evans seemed to lose track of what he was saying, and then went on—"that, well, the pay isn't much, you know, and they always do need trained workers so badly, but so few people go into it because of the low salaries, and Ruth felt that people who—who didn't need to work for the money ought to— She was a very serious girl."

And she'd been the only child. "I see," said Maddox. And there just could be something there. A social worker would have been seeing all sorts and conditions of people. "She worked downtown?"

"What? Oh yes, the County Welfare—it's on Temple, I think."

Mrs. Goldfarb stopped sobbing with a final hiccup and said in a thick voice, "Benny. There was that man Wedeck." She was a small fat woman with a mustache, and now she looked up from her sodden handkerchief. She had the most beautiful dark eyes Maddox had ever seen, great sad eyes with long thick lashes.

"I'd almost forgot that," said Goldfarb slowly. "But I guess it'd be damned farfetched. That he'd do such a thing."

"Wedeck, Mr. Goldfarb? Ronnie'd had a quarrel with him?"

"Well, my God, it was months ago. Who'd do such a— Well, it wasn't Ronnie's fault, not a bit, it was all this Wedeck's fault, see. I don't remember his first name—"

"It was Harry, Benny."

"Yeah, I guess so. See, he's one of the ones Ronnie did his tax figuring for him. That was a way he earned as he could, all the time the doctors were still working on the leg. It was sort of seasonal, of course—he had other jobs too, last couple of years—small firms just have a bookkeeper in a day or so a week. Joe left him a little stock, he had about fifteen hundred a year income, and with that and what he could earn outside—"

"He was awfully mad at Ronnie that time," said the woman.

"When he knew it was all his own fault! Listen, it's crazy! To shoot him, all this time later? And not care if he shot somebody else too? I don't— Well, what it was, Sergeant, Ronnie figured his tax for him.The damn income tax. Matter o' fact he used to do mine too, only he didn't charge me. I never could make head or tail— Well, I guess this Wedeck, who I seem to remember has a drugstore or something around where Ronnie was living, wasn't an awful businesslike guy, and he forgot to give Ronnie some figures, I think it was some real estate he'd sold, a lot or something, and so of course Ronnie never figured it in the rest of his gross that year—that'd be last year, and Wedeck's gross I mean—and pretty soon the tax boys came down on him for it. Because all the snooping around they do these days, it showed up."

"When was this? The tax estimate Ronnie figured for him would be the January one?"

"That's right. I guess it was May or June when the tax boys came around—maybe even July." The woman sobbed again.

And that was something too. "He blamed Ronnie? I suppose they slapped a fine on him?"

"I dunno, I guess so. Yeah, he tried to maintain he did give Ronnie all the figures, and it was Ronnie slipped up. But Ronnie always had his head screwed on pretty tight—like Joe he was that way—and he'd kept every last thing Wedeck gave him, so he could show it was all Wedeck's fault. But Wedeck was mad, he said. But I just don't see— To shoot—my God. And poor Ruth too. I just can't take it in. They were two fine young people. Sergeant—"

"Yes?" said Maddox.

Goldfarb was breathing heavily. He struck one fist on the

arm of his chair. "The things go on nowadays, who's surprised at what happens, some people. Some people. I mean, you get young folk on this dope, and running around God knows where, and drinking and carrying on. Some reason, kids like that get in trouble, even get killed! But Ronnie and Ruth! Serious, ambitious, hardworking, respectable young people. Nobody either of 'em knew'd be the kind— It just doesn't make sense, Sergeant! No sense at all!"

It looked funny, all right. Only, probably, until they looked a little deeper. Ruth and Ronnie might have been very respectable young people, but they had been young, and conceivably could have been mixed into something the Evanses and Goldfarbs didn't know about.

When Maddox left, he surveyed the murder scene outside with interest. Somebody, by all the evidence, had had it in for Ronnie, or Ruth, or both of them. Rowan had collected what evidence there was: there wasn't much.

On the east side of the Evanses' house a tall privet hedge separated their property from the house next door. The driveway was on that side, right next to the hedge. The lot was a deep one and it was a long, fairly steep drive: all of the houses along here sat a good way up from the street, beyond terraced lawns. About forty feet up from the street, on the other side of the tall hedge, was where X had lain in wait.

How long, who could say? There was a tree there, with a flower bed around its trunk; in the bed were a lot of blurred footprints—nothing good enough to take moulages of, but the householders had been questioned and said the bed had been intact late that afternoon. So. There'd been two cigarette butts; the lab had them now. The hedge was tall, but not so tall that an average-height man couldn't have fired over it; that was apparently what he'd done.

He? More likely a man, though you never knew.

And Ruth had been a social worker. Well. They came good, bad, and indifferent like other people: the good ones were invaluable, but they were few and far between.

He sat behind the wheel of the Frazer-Nash and looked at the pictures Evans and the Goldfarbs had given him. One of Ronnie and Ruth together, and a salon portrait of Ruth. He looked at them and he felt a little cold and sad because, whatever kind of people they had been, they were dead, and that was the ultimate finality.

Twenty-five and twenty-seven. Sometimes you wondered if there was Anything doing any planning at all, or if everything just happened at random.

Morgenstern a good-looking young fellow. High forehead, intelligent eyes under heavy brows, a good jaw, a well-cut wide mouth. Ruth had been something of a beauty in a quiet way. Long dark hair to her shoulders, large eyes, probably blue or gray, an oval face, slim arched brows, a mouth made for smiling.

Neither of them looked like the kind to get mixed into something dubious. They looked like responsible people. Their records said they had been.

Maddox sighed and put the pictures away. He looked up the drive again. So, only two of five slugs in Ruth's body; the surgeon hadn't said how many in Morgenstern's. Three slugs missing at least. If the ones from the bodies weren't intact enough to be identified, they'd have to do some crawling around up there in the hope of finding others. Standing behind that hedge, X would have fired diagonally, toward the car (windows open? yes, probably), and those slugs would have gone, again probably, diagonally down the terraced lawn toward the street. Or, if any of them had been deflected by passing through the bodies, almost anywhere. Maddox sighed again.

It was after twelve; he drove down to the Grotto on Santa Monica Boulevard, where a good many of the Wilcox Street men lunched, and found D'Arcy and Rodriguez there before him. Lank dark D'Arcy's seventy-six inches were draped gracelessly into a chair and he was staring into a Scotch and water. Dapper, mustached Rodriguez was poring over the last pages of *The Reader Is Warned*.

Maddox sat down at the table with them. Rodriguez started and looked up. "You get anything?"

"Don't know—some places to look." The waitress came up and he said he'd have a Scotch and water and the usual steak.

"The Ballistics report came up," said Rodriguez. "It was a Smith and Wesson 1950 army revolver—forty-five ACP cartridges. A cannon."

"Oh really," said Maddox. "What load does that carry? Six or seven cartridges, I think six. Anyway, not more. So he stopped to reload. What does that say? That he meant to get them both?"

"I wouldn't say necessarily," said D'Arcy. He took a long swallow of his drink and got out a cigarette. "Look, Ivor, they were engaged." He looked a little sour, probably thinking of his lost love Margaret Talmadge. "They'd just come back off a date. They weren't sitting there in the front seat discussing nuclear physics. And, so X was only about ten feet off, but it was dark. He could have just been aiming at Morgenstern, or just at the girl, and got both because they were necking."

"Um," said Maddox. "Funny thing is, by what I've heard so far, this pair could have been sitting there talking about nuclear physics. Or politics. Or sociology. I don't know. See what we get from people their own age who knew them. What did you get at L.A.C.C., César?"

"Nothing that I can see points anywhere. Morgenstern took three day classes, Mondays, Wednesdays, and Fridays, and four night classes. He was a good student. Everybody liked him—everybody very shocked to hear about the murder. At least nobody seems to have actively disliked him. But you know, a college like L.A.C.C., it's not like the average college—the students don't have such close contact. About ninety percent of all the students going there, they're working their way through, maybe going just part time, and there isn't the—the extracurricular campus stuff, the clubs and so on. Your average L.A.C.C. student—" and Rodriguez should know, Maddox thought, as he'd had a couple of years there himself—"is a pretty serious student from a fairly low income group. Not so much interested in the campus frolics and fraternities and so on, as in actual classes. So unless Morgenstern had a couple of personal buddies there—which didn't show up—it could be nobody there knew him very well, he was just another student. I saw all his instructors. None of them thought he had any real close friends in his classes. I got some names of other students he'd had lunch with, like that. Kind of interesting, every single one of those—mmh—" he grinned—"in the nonsuperior-white-Protestant category."

"Oh?" said Maddox. The waitress brought his drink and he sampled it.

"I'd say a good fifty percent of the student body there is Negro now. Nice and encouraging. And a lot of the rest Mexican, Oriental, and all sorts of mixtures. By what I got, Morgenstern seems to have singled out a couple of the Negroes in his classes, others like that. But on the other hand, most of the student body being what's so tactfully called from minority groups, that may have been just coincidence."

"Sure," said Maddox.

"I'm afraid," said D'Arcy, "that pig is going to get in the papers. Damn fool thing. I don't know how these press boys get wind of things. Laidlaw collared me—the *Times* boy. When I told him the Humane Society had the pig he said he'd chase a photographer right down to Ann Street."

"Oh well," said Maddox. Thinking about the pink pig, he laughed.

"I've got a hunch—" began D'Arcy; and Sergeant Ellis came up and pulled out the fourth chair at the table.

"—goddamned tenderhearted judges!" he said bitterly. "And splitting hairs about the letter of the law! But I swear I'll get that bastard good, and damn the State Supreme Court! Bring me a double rye."

"Yes sir, Sergeant." The waitress hurried off.

"You said it was a vice thing," said Maddox. "What's the trouble, George?"

"Trouble!" said Ellis. "That smug bastard sitting there. I swear to God he's running a string of call girls, and probably a damn big string too. But that goddamn court ruling on resorting— I've got nothing to charge him on and no remote legal reason to get a search warrant, damn it. This Howard William Cleveland. He's got a pedigree—downtown and back in Philadelphia—procuring, resorting, pimping. Right now he owns and manages this little hotel out on Fairfax. All open and legal as you please, and I'd take an oath on a stack of

Bibles he's got some of his girls stashed there and probably a lot more elsewhere, and can I prove it? I just *know*, but I've got no evidence, and no reason to ask for a search warrant."

"Difficult," agreed Maddox. "I know. But if I know you, George, you're not just giving up on it. What are you doing?"

Ellis grunted and downed half of his rye. "Daisy Hoffman's going to nose around and try to get acquainted with some of the—" he snorted—"young single women living there."

"Oh," said Maddox. "Well, a sort of forlorn hope. That kind learn to be cagey." Also, he thought, as good a policewoman as she was, Sergeant Daisy Hoffman—even in civilian dress—smelled of the Law. He had the small beginning of an idea about Ellis's problem, and being uninterested let it slide. Because, hell, there that kind were, you couldn't legislate against human nature.

His steak arrived and he started on it.

"By the way," said Ellis, "Donaldson said something—about a pig. What the hell, in the middle of town?"

"Oh my God, that pig," said Rodriguez, and started laughing.

"I have a hunch," said D'Arcy with gloomy relish, "that we're going to hear more from whoever left that pig there. Practical joke, yah." He finished his drink.

"What about the pig?" asked Ellis interestedly. Rodriguez started to tell him, still laughing.

"So what did you get on the shooting?" D'Arcy asked Maddox. "You didn't say."

"A couple of people to see—couple of places to look. I want," said Maddox, rattling ice cubes in his glass, "to talk to a fellow named Wedeck first."

Three

RODRIGUEZ WENT DOWNTOWN TO SEE THE PEOPLE AT THE WELfare office; Maddox and D'Arcy went out to Ardmore Avenue where Morgenstern had lived, to cover that. Goldfarb had said this Wedeck had a store of some kind near there: try to locate him too.

Morgenstern had (like Maddox) rented a little frame house on the rear of the lot behind a larger house: Mrs. Barker's house. They rang her bell first, and when she let them in she was crying gently. "I heard it on the TV news—about Ronnie! It's just too awful. I couldn't believe it! And his poor girl too. It don't bear thinking about! He showed me her picture—a real sweet-looking girl."

She answered questions readily, ramblingly. Ronnie had lived there for nearly four years, he was friendly, lots of people around here knew him. She gave him something off the rent because he mowed the lawn, like that, so he'd got acquainted with the neighbors. And he'd shopped for himself at the little market round on Melrose. She knew all his circumstances, as Goldfarb had detailed; she'd been so happy for him when he got engaged to Ruth. "He was Jewish, you know, but he didn't

— 24

go to church, the temple I mean. Not that I ever knew. He was such a friendly, nice boy—who'd want to do a terrible thing like that? And that sweet girl—"

No, he hadn't had people come to visit much. A few times some of the other students from the college, some of them black, but Mrs. Barker judged people as people and they'd seemed to be nice quiet fellows. No wild parties, no drinking or maybe only some beer, and not to be getting tight. Besides, Ronnie'd had to be careful with money. "He was already saving up, for the honeymoon and to open an office. Just don't bear thinking of."

"Did he go around with other girls before he met Ruth?" asked Maddox. Evidently Ronnie had confided in his maternal-looking landlady.

"Some—not an awful lot, he didn't have the money to be taking girls out much. Even if they just went to a movie or something, and a snack afterward, it'd be four-five dollars, you know. . . . No sir, he never brought any girls here. Yes, there was a girl named Loretta, she went to the college too, and he wasn't going steady with her, about the same time he'd sometimes go out with a girl named Kitty, but after he met Ruth he never dated other girls. He was real serious about her right from the start, and he used to talk to me about it. You know —first off he was afraid she wouldn't think about marrying him because he was Jewish, and then later on when he knew that wouldn't make a difference, he was worried because her family has a good deal of money and maybe they'd think it was that reason he wanted to marry her. Anybody knew Ronnie— But it all worked out fine, when he'd met her folks and they saw what a really nice young man he was, and so ambitious and all. And after they got engaged, her folks had his aunt and uncle to dinner, and it was all— Oh dear, and to think what it's all come to." Her face crumpled again.

"Mrs. Barker, we'd like to look through his place." They had the key; there hadn't been anything in his pockets but the usual, expectable things.

"Oh dear, I suppose. Though I don't know what you'd expect to find to tell you anything. Nobody could have had any reason to— Ronnie! Why—" She was leading them around the side of the house, to the little low frame house in the rear— "when I told Mrs. Kaufmann next door, she cried too. And as for old Mr. Rhys, why, I can just imagine how he'll be feeling—if he knows about it yet. That'll show you what a kind, thoughtful young chap Ronnie was, Officer. He used to put himself out, like, for the old man—sorry for him, you know— he'd go and play checkers with him, and bring him magazines, like that. Mr. Rhys is retired, on pension, and all sole alone, no family—he's got the artheritis. Well, I don't know what you expect to find here, but—"

They didn't know either. It was just one of the places to look.

It was a neat little three-roomed place, with shabby rugs, old but comfortable furniture; if Morgenstern hadn't had quite so many books as Maddox, there were plenty—a lot of reference books, of course, and legal texts. There was a good portable phonograph and a stack of classical records. There was a small desk in the living room, and they went through that minutely, but there wasn't anything significant in it— just some recent homework, a neat notebook full of notes on lectures in a fine small handwriting, a couple of letters from Goldfarb—apparently, though they lived within visiting distance, they corresponded; probably Ronnie's busy schedule didn't allow for many trips way out to Duarte. There was an address book with not too many names in it; they'd all be checked out. And there was, in several thick 8½ x 11 manila envelopes, a lot of financial records of the various people he'd done tax work for, within the last three years. Ronnie a very careful fellow.

There was nothing to give any hint about anybody who might have wanted Ronnie dead. Just the shabby neat living quarters of a rather poor young man. In the little kitchen, modest supplies: a cheap bottle of red wine in the cupboard, a six-pack of beer in the tiny refrigerator, with bread, milk, eggs, bacon. In the standing wardrobe in the little bedroom, two suits (he'd have been wearing his best one on the date), a couple of pairs of slacks, miscellaneous working clothes, shoes. Nothing in any of the pockets. In the bureau, a few shirts, socks, underwear, handkerchiefs: a laundry bag with a dirty shirt, a pair of shorts, an undershirt, and a pair of socks in it. He'd have done his own laundry at the nearest Laundromat.

"And you know," said Maddox ruminatively, "the fact that they were shot outside *Ruth's* home rather makes it look as if she was the intended victim—or both of them, of course. Because if X was just after Ronnie, well, this is just as handy a spot to lay in wait for him, isn't it? I wouldn't doubt that Mrs. Barker goes to bed early, the front house'd be all dark. Ronnie wouldn't leave lights on here, to burn up money. It'd be damn dark on that little walk out there."

"I don't know," said D'Arcy, rubbing his long jaw. "Sort of pay your money, take your choice, isn't it? These lots are a damn sight narrower than those up on Franklin—neighbors a lot closer, every side. He mightn't have found it so easy to get away so fast, after doing the shooting."

"That's so." Maddox was looking gloomy too, now. "Right now, D'Arcy, I'm more sold on the idea that Ruth was the one X was after. See what César gets about her recent cases. There is, of course, this Wedeck." Harry Wedeck, Mrs. Barker had said, ran the little pharmacy around on Melrose Avenue. She'd heard about the "little fuss" he'd had with Ronnie but didn't figure there was much in it. All his own fault, which he'd come to see. "Don't answer the question, Enough motive? Depends on who's got the motive, doesn't it?"

"Human nature being what it is. We'd better go see him."

They locked the door after them and went to see Wedeck.

Wedeck looked quite normal. It was the typical neighborhood drugstore, an independent, a little shabby, a little cluttered, probably a small goldmine to its owner; it looked as if it had been here for years. Wedeck was a sallow-faced big man in his fifties, with thinning dark hair and a friendly manner, which receded a little when he heard who they were and what they wanted. But he didn't seem nervous—just incredulous.

"Yes, so you've heard about that— My God, to think of a nice young couple like that getting murdered! Well, for God's sake, you're not thinking I had anything to— Over that?" He shrugged. "Look, sure, I had that hassle with Morgenstern. I admit it, I sort of flew off the handle when the damn tax fellows came down on me, because I could've sworn on my life I'd given Morgenstern every single last figure, see? So I thought right then, serves me right, trying save a little money, get this college boy figure it for me instead of a regular tax expert, see, though I knew a couple of people he'd done it for and they had no beef, said he was a smart fellow, so I thought— And I kind of blew off at him, sure. It was back in July. See, it was a Saturday just like today and the damn tax men looking like they were figuring haul me off to jail any minute, and I shut the store and took them straight up to where Morgenstern lived and he was home, and— But he'd kept all the papers on it, and I didn't *believe* it because I was so damn sure I'd given him everything, but—"

"You got a fine?"

"I did," said Wedeck bitterly. "Those damn bloodhounds, asking me for an accounting of my money—throwing millions away, all this damn foreign aid."

Cops in public aren't supposed to have any politics, so neither Maddox nor D'Arcy replied to that one. "So what were you doing and where were you at one A.M. this morning?" asked Maddox.

"Me?" said Wedeck incredulously. "You can't think *I'd* have— My God, last July, and I had to admit it was my fault."

"Where?" asked Maddox.

"Well, for God's sake, I was home in bed with my wife," said Wedeck. "Asleep. We were home all evening, looking at TV. We had a snack about ten thirty and then we went to bed. Well, I took a bath first. I have trouble sleeping sometimes, and I find a hot bath before I retire—"

"Your wife a pretty good sleeper? Take a pill or anything?"

"No," said Wedeck stiffly. "I guess we were both asleep by midnight or before. You can't think *I*—"

Maddox didn't really think so. But on Ronnie, it was looking even funnier: nice, quiet, respectable young fellow, living within his income, respectable family, no known enemies. . . . "I'm still liking Ruth," he said to D'Arcy. "Just a little bit more likely, considering where she worked." He looked at his watch; it was nearly four o'clock. "Let's go back to base and see if César turned up anything."

Rodriguez had something, all right. He'd seen Ruth Evans's immediate superior, a Mrs. Bertha Hardwick— "Old-timer down there, I'd say, hard as nails, she's heard and seen it all, good at her job. You'd always know where you stood with her anyway—you know the type. Very much shocked about Ruth —even more shocked to think the reason for it might go back to her job. But she saw *that* right away, and parted like a lamb. Said Ruth was a very good worker, young but learning all the time. Serious girl."

"We knew that."

"*Vaya despacio,* I'm getting to the important part. As you don't need telling, they're always carrying quite a case load, every social worker they've got, and Ruth was no exception. Just lately—" Rodriguez flipped open his notebook—"she'd been dealing with about a dozen families on relief, various troubles like potential school drop-outs, and alcoholic husbands—*and* wives—and so on. Also, this Mrs. Ritter, who is on relief and wants a divorce from her husband. Ruth was helping her on that, advising her and so on. Ritter doesn't want a divorce—had accused Ruth of persuading his wife to leave him. Ritter," said Rodriguez, "has just come home on parole from Quentin. Second count of armed robbery, a three-to-five."

"Be damned," said D'Arcy.

"I like Mr. Ritter," said Maddox. "He sounds promising."

"I thought so," agreed Rodriguez. "I can also offer you one Thomas Wales. Ruth had been working with that family too. Gist of it is, the mother's dead, there are six kids and Wales is a part-time laborer, part-time drunk. Oldest girl is nineteen, been trying to support the family, keep some sort of home, and she seems to be a bright girl, wants an education, and Ruth had been working on her trying to get her to spend some of her money on herself, go to college or at least night classes. Wales was mad as hell about it—half the time he steals the girl's earnings to go off on a spree. He'd sworn at Ruth, accused her of interfering, like that."

"Um," said Maddox. "He have a pedigree?"

"What else? Little stuff—petty larceny, a few brawls in bars, D.-and-D."

"Well. Tell on," said Maddox, eyeing Rodriguez's expression.

"Pues sí. Another family she'd been helping—trying to— have got a schizo son. Oldest one—eighteen. He spent a couple of years at Camarillo. Mother's one of these doting fond mamas—ignorant people, you know, don't know about that kind of thing, and I expect the damn-fool head doctors talking the jargon to them which even educated people can't always translate. Anyway, mama's convinced poor Eddy's really all right, her baby, the doctors have cured him, and she gives her husband no peace until they get Eddy home again. It is," said Rodriguez, "a funny sort of thing, but you know how that kind often do settle down meek as little lambs once they're tucked away, when they throw tantrums on any excuse at home. I suppose in this case mama's indulgence has something to do with that. And they're always strapped for space up there, and they let Eddy come home. Yes, they're on relief. Well, as you can imagine, Eddy at home isn't so good for the other two kids, both younger, he'd pulled some tantrums and they can't study, can't have friends in, and so on. And Ruth had been trying to make mama understand that, grasp the fact that schizos just get progressively worse and can't be cured, and that it's best for everybody he should be sent to Camarillo again. And I suppose Eddy would have heard her saying so."

"Yes," said Maddox. "A schizo. Does he have sense enough to realize what she was talking about? Where do they live? Access to a car—a gun? Could he get away alone long enough?"

Rodriguez shrugged. "It's just a possibility. Personally I like Ritter. Or, a little less possible, Wales."

"So do I. Let's put out a call on both of them."

"I already have."

"That's my bright boy," said Maddox. This might be quite simple after all. A crude one, if it had been Ritter or Wales. The kind they so often got. Yes.

Those calls had just gone out unless Ritter and Wales were peacefully at their home addresses, they probably wouldn't be picked up right away.

He went down the hall to the coffee and Coke dispenser, and ran into Ellis filling a Dixie cup with coffee. "Your call-girl thing," he said, feeling amiable (always so nice when a thing turned out rather routine—you could always get the excitement of something complex, without all the work on it, vicariously in the detective novels—as César had discovered).

"Oh, I don't expect results on that for a while, way we're having to work it," said Ellis.

Maddox held a cup under the dispenser and pressed the button. "Little shortcut maybe. Just an idea."

"Don't tell me you've got an idea."

"The type of setup you said it was. Sure. Take the youngest and best-looking female we've got, which would be, obviously,

Sue Carstairs. Put her in a sexy cocktail dress and a lot of make-up with the latest crazy hairdo, and let her register at that hotel. Cleveland's hotel, where he owns and manages and probably has some of his girls stashed. Let her sit around the bar there—there *is* a bar?"

"Sure—grill and cocktail lounge."

"O.K." Maddox drank coffee, and said, "Damn paper cups. So then you take us—all the plain-clothes men on duty—and maybe a few uniformed men you put in civilian dress, see. And one by one we show up there, all very obviously—um— make assignations with an obvious just-starting-out call girl. One by one we go up to her room, stay half an hour, an hour, and how's Cleveland to know we're sitting up there playing checkers or talking about the latest best seller?"

"I don't get it," said Ellis.

"Well, with Cleveland's record," said Maddox, "and our Sue could probably fix herself up to be quite an eyeful—I'd lay you maybe even money, George, that within a week Cleveland might make some fatherly attempt to rope her into his own string. And I have heard tell of these miniature tape recorders you can wear under your shirt, I suppose Sue could tuck one inside her bra."

Ellis stared at him. "My God. Maddox the brain. That *is* a hell of an idea, Ivor."

"If you're being so damn conscientious about the letter of the law," said Maddox, grinning, "and so determined to catch up to your boy. Me, I figure what the hell, on that kind. There they are."

"You would. That *is* an idea."

"Carstairs won't like it," said Maddox, "but she'll play. Our Sue you can rely on." He supposed he liked Policewoman

Carstairs so much because she was about the only young, good-looking female he knew who didn't fall all over him and bat her eyelashes at him every time they ran into each other. Nice reliable Carstairs, he thought comfortably.

"Hell, that *is* an idea," said Ellis thoughtfully. "Thanks very much."

Maddox went home—neither Ritter nor Wales had been picked up by six thirty—took a shower, shaved and dressed again, in a clean shirt and his newest tie, and—with foreboding —went to Dulcie's party.

It was quite a party. Dulcie was quite a girl. And it all turned out even as he had known it would. Damn it, so he was an L.A.P.D. man, that didn't automatically stop him being also a human male aged thirty-one. Dulcie—well—

"But you *will* stay on, Ivor darling? Haven't seen you in ages."

And, my God, suppose Ritter or Wales had been picked up, there was an Urgent on it—and the office tried to get him? Oh well.

He got home, to the little frame house behind the Clintons' house on Gregory Avenue, at three thirty A.M. His day off this month was Tuesday; the alarm woke him at seven ten and he got out of bed with a groan and dragged himself to the bathroom.

He got to Wilcox Street at five to eight, and found the office empty except for D'Arcy, who was on the phone.

"A what? Oh— But for God's sake, I don't— Well, all right, I'll come and look at it. Morning," said D'Arcy, putting the phone down. "Late night?"

"God," said Maddox.

"I told you we'd hear more from him. Come on."

"Who?"

"That practical joker. The pig. This one's out on Detroit Avenue. Stoner got the call again. Let's go see what it is. I gather there's quite a hassle going on."

"Oh, for God's sake." With this homicide—

They drove out to Detroit Avenue. This one was a bit more subtle than the pink pig, it turned out.

They found Stoner attempting to soothe a man and a woman. The woman was incoherent with fury, and the man was incoherent with rapturous hilarity.

Mr. and Mrs. Michael Foster, people in their forties, the woman very neat and dowdy in a powder-blue rayon dress and a very matronly hat, the man in a sober navy-blue suit and dark tie. They had—Stoner had got some information—come out to the garage at about seven thirty to drive to church, the eight o'clock service, and discovered that the driveway gate was entirely blocked by an enormous and mysterious carton with a neatly wrapped small parcel on top of it.

Mr. Michael Foster was almost, but not quite, speechless. "Oh my God—but it's *priceless!* Just *priceless!* Somebody knows Marion, all right—knows her but good! Oh my God, I'll die laughing. Talk about *housekeepers!* Scrubbing all the floors with Lysol every week. I can't sit down in the living room without I take a bath and brush my damn teeth—wax the kitchen floor every day. Oh my God, I'll die— Got to have a dishwasher so the dishes all get sterilized. Somebody knows Marion, all right. Time and again I tell her—but that woman—"

"Sir," said Stoner uneasily, "I don't see—"

Foster waved a feeble arm, doubled over with mirth.

The obstruction placed during the night across the Fosters' driveway consisted of a large carton containing no less than a gross of gallon bottles of a popular antiseptic cleaning agent. The neat parcel on top of it contained a book. The book was a recent edition of *The Works of Sigmund Freud*.

Four

IT WAS NO PART OF THE POLICE DEPARTMENT'S DUTY, BUT WHEN Foster had got himself under control, Maddox and D'Arcy helped him shove the enormous carton up the drive and into the garage. The woman, red-faced with fury, had gone into the house, slamming the back door after her. "My God, I wish I knew who did it." Foster was still chortling. "Hell of a joke. *Priceless*. That woman." He straightened and wiped his brow. "Not that I think a real subtle little hint like this is going to change her character overnight. I sometimes do wonder why I've stayed with her for sixteen years." They left him looking thoughtfully from the carton to the back door of the house.

"Same joker, all right," said D'Arcy. "Kind of the same earmarks, you might say. We're not far from Higman Avenue."

"About five blocks. I'll tell you something else, D'Arcy, It's an adult, not kids. And it could be more than one. Because that was a big pig." The Sunday editions would have been made up already, but doubtless the pig would appear in all the papers tomorrow, human interest—"and that carton was damn heavy. Both those little jokes took some care and planning, didn't they? Both were done at night—or more likely very early morning—and whoever it was had to move damn quiet, not to wake those people up. I think it's likely he's got a pickup truck."

"Well, I see he had to be careful and plan it out, but one man could have got that carton up there if he had one of those dollies. And to go to such trouble, just for a little laugh—" D'Arcy shook his head.

"That type of mind," said Maddox, "never thinks anything is too much trouble. And whoever it is, he knows both the Endlers and the Fosters." Foster had disclaimed knowing the Endlers.

"Somebody in the neighborhood. People!" said D'Arcy disgustedly. "Don't they think we've got anything more important to do than chase down a damn-fool practical joker?"

"Well, he's not really doing much harm," said Maddox inattentively. He was, naturally, a good deal more concerned about the X on Ronnie and Ruth than about who had delivered the pink pig and was evidently busy thinking up other pranks.

"Look," said D'Arcy suddenly, "ask the company that makes that stuff who bought a gross of gallon bottles lately. That should show."

"I think this joker is playing it a little cuter than that. We can ask, of course."

When they got back to the office, a little information had drifted in. He had asked Records (forlorn hope) if Ritter or Wales had gun permits. Neither of them had. Naturally. He had sent down all the male names out of Ruth Evans's address book: none of those had permits either. They had found Frank Gates's name there; some time today he wanted to see Gates. The phone book was modestly crowded with Phil Delgados and Bob Pierces, but they'd track those down in time. Just the routine, to look everywhere.

Maddox didn't think much of the schizophrenic boy, but as a last resort—

O'Brien and Donaldson were out hunting for Ritter and Wales, and at nine ten O'Brien called in. Plodding, stupid, well-meaning, elderly O'Brien.

"Say, I located this Ritter for you, Sarge."

It annoyed Maddox to be called Sarge. "Yes," he said gently. "Where?"

"He's to home. Where he lives. Down on San Pedro downtown. I mean, you give me the address, I come to see first is he here, and he ain't, but while I'm talking to the manager o' the place, a guy comes in and goes upstairs and the manager says that's him. You want I should pick him up and bring him in?"

"No," said Maddox after a moment, "I think I'd like to have a look round his place. Stay there and collar him if he tries to leave. I'll be there in twenty minutes."

"O.K., Sarge," said O'Brien obediently.

Maddox collected Rodriguez and they started downtown in the Frazer-Nash. Rodriguez was silent all the way, buried in a paperback copy of Like Love. Having come late to the field as a mystery fan, Rodriguez still had a lot of catching up to do; and Maddox was still feeling a little sleepy.

The address on San Pedro was an ancient rooming house, a ramshackle frame in best General Grant style, with gingerbread still brave around its eaves. It needed a coat of paint. A scrawny old man was sitting on the porch in a rocking chair. He had on red suspenders over a mended woolen undershirt. "Are you the manager here?" asked Maddox.

"Sure am." He spat tobacco juice over the porch railing.

"We're looking for Mr. Ritter."

"Mmh," said the old man wisely. "More fuzz like the guy inside. Sure. He's room number five, left at the top o' the stairs." He was still rocking placidly when they went in.

O'Brien was waiting at the top of the stairs. "He's still in, Sarge."

"O.K." Maddox knocked on the door and after a moment it was opened.

Joseph Ritter, just out of Quentin for the second time, was a big dark fellow. His hair grew so low on his forehead that he might have had no forehead at all, but he was good looking otherwise, regular features, blue eyes. He was about six two and built like Tarzan, with wide muscled shoulders and a lean waist and flat hips. He was wearing a pair of white undershorts and a sleeveless T-shirt; no need to pat him down, no concealed weapons there. He blinked at them, and at the badge in Maddox's hand, and then smiled an unpleasant smile.

"The fuzz," he said. "A guy has a count on him, every time a caper gets pulled they come and try to beat out a confession. I'm clean. I done nothing, cop."

"Well, we'd just like to have a little talk with you and be sure," said Maddox. "In, Ritter. You mind if we have a look around here?"

"Help yourself," said Ritter instantly; which didn't sound encouraging. Rodriguez raised his brows at Maddox and began to go through the drawers in the single bureau beside the sagging bed; Maddox sat down in the one straight chair and motioned Ritter to the bed, and O'Brien stood stolid and beefy against the door.

"So what the hell's it all about? I'm clean, reported to the P.A. officer yesterday."

"Ruth Evans," said Maddox, watching him. Ritter's expression didn't change.

"So, who the hell is Ruth Evans?" Then his mouth tightened. "Oh," he said. "I saw a thing in the papers—she got shot, didn't she? With some guy. Well, for Jesus's sweet sake, bloodhound, I didn't know her, never heard of her, why the hell you—"

"Oh yes, you did, Ritter. I understand your wife's getting a divorce from you?"

Again the man's face tightened, to grim and bitter anger. "I'll say the hell she is. I love that dame, I never spoke a cross word at her, anything she wanted she always got, and the kid too. She's got no call to— But I argue at her till I'm black in the face, she— It was all that goddamned old maid social worker's fault!—got after her, feeds her all this damn crap, make a better background for the kid on her own, I'm a— That goddamned—"

"Yes," said Maddox. "Ruth Evans. The social worker, Ritter."

For a moment Ritter just stared at him. Rodriguez was in the closet now. "What the hell are you giving me, cop?" asked Ritter roughly. "You trying snow me or something? That young girl got shot? Ruth—"

"Are you trying to tell me," asked Maddox, "that you didn't know who she was? This woman you're convinced persuaded your wife to leave you? You didn't even know her name?"

"No, I didn't. Why the hell should I? I know what she was all the time tellin' Lynnie, is all, damn snoopy bastards from

41 —

the damn Welfare come stick their paws in people's private lives—just because Lynnie got sick one time while I was still in the pen, and asked for help."

"Now just wait a minute here," said Maddox. "You heard all about what the social worker said to your wife, and you never once heard her name? Your wife never said, 'Well, Miss Evans told me,' and so on?"

"Well, for Christ's sweet sake, suppose the hell she did? There're millions of people named Evans. I still think you're tryina snow me, cop. I saw a picture, that girl got shot. Her, a social worker down the Welfare? Livin' in a big house like that? Don't tell—"

"How d'you know what her house looked like?"

"There was a picture of that in the paper too. I don't—"

"Well, not all social workers these days are dowdy old maids," said Maddox. "So let's hear what you were up to on Friday night."

"Friday— For God's sake, try to tie me in to a thing like this. Friday. My God, how'd I—"

"It's only a couple of days ago," said Maddox. "Where were you that evening?"

Ritter thought, looking down at his hands. Finally he said, still looking angry, "I went to dinner at the Hi Lo Café down the street. I ran into a couple of pals there."

"Who?"

"Uh—Dan Reilly and Bill Prince. So sure, sure, they both done a little time too, what the hell's that say? Damn P.A. rules—what's a guy supposed to do, just to stay out, forget everybody he ever knew?"

Some of the rules were, of course, a little unrealistic. "Where'd you go from there?"

"Uh—"

"You've already admitted violating one rule, boy," said Maddox. "Associating with known criminals. I suppose you're a little leery of confessing further that you went into a bar—another violation—and had some drinks. Which bar?"

"For Christ's sweet sake," snarled Ritter, "isn't a guy supposed to be human, he's been in the pen? Isn't a guy— Oh my God." He dragged a hand over his face. "Casey's down on Third."

"And how long were you there?"

"Until about midnight," said Ritter sullenly.

"And then where?"

"Nowhere. Here. I come back here and went to bed. That's level. No, I didn't see anybody else lives here and nobody saw me come in, I guess, but—"

Maddox looked at him in silence for a moment and then said, "Well, we'll see. You stay right around the neighborhood and be a good boy, hm?"

"You damn guys—now they'll probably haul me in off P.A.!" said Ritter.

Downstairs, the old man was gone. "Not a smell of anything funny," said Rodriguez. "No gun."

"Um," said Maddox. A man with a record like Ritter's usually had some kind of gun around; but it could be a pal was holding it for him, while he was on parole. It could also be that he'd had a gun—up to last Friday night, or rather early Saturday morning—and had prudently got rid of it after shooting Ruth and Ronnie.

"And," said Rodriguez, "no alibi."

"I don't know," said Maddox, thinking of how Ritter's eyes had shifted. "Could be he has—maybe he picked up a girl or something—and isn't saying because if it was something like that—or a crap game, say—he would be hauled in off parole."

"In a homicide case, he isn't speaking up if he's alibied?"

"Taking the chance. I don't know, I do like him for it, but—" Maddox looked at O'Brien and sighed. "Look, let's try to tie him up to a gun. O'Brien, you go hunt up those two he said he was with." He wrote the names down for him. "Records over at Headquarters will have addresses on them. Ask to look around where they're living, make them a little nervous. O.K.? I'll send Donaldson down when he comes in—take a look at all Ritter's known pals you can locate—the barkeeps around here'll likely give you a few names."

"O.K.," said O'Brien, and turned and started off.

"He's bound to retire sometime," said Rodriguez. "And we'll get some nice bright boy who's been through the police academy."

"But when?" said Maddox. They got into the Frazer-Nash. "I think we want to see Mrs. Ritter."

"Good idea."

They got a little there. Lynn Ritter was a cut above her husband; she had a pretty little blonde girl about three and didn't look much over twenty herself. She hadn't known about Ritter's record when she married him. Well, he was a good-looking big hunk of man: understandable, maybe. She admitted he'd always been good to her, but she just couldn't feel the same after she knew his record, and found he didn't hold a regular job and all. It was the uncertainty of it, never knowing when he'd pull something and get dropped on. She looked at them with troubled blue eyes and said she'd talked it over with Miss Evans a lot, Miss Evans had been nice. She'd told Lynn it was about a thousand to one against a fellow like Joe ever getting reformed, and probably sooner or later he'd get Lynn in trouble with him, and then what about the baby? She'd be a lot wiser just to cut her losses.

"Joe was awfully mad about it," she said, "but—"

Well, yes, she'd probably mentioned Miss Evans's name to him, because she'd told him some of what Miss Evans had said, trying to explain. Just awful Miss Evans getting killed like that, but for goodness' sake, they didn't think Joe—

"You said he was angry about it. At her. Do you think he was angry enough for that?"

She looked down at the floor. "I—I—don't know," she said in a low voice.

"So?" said Rodriguez as they came away. "Not very hard for him to find out her first name. He's not a big brain, but he's not an idiot either. Call her office, ask, have you a Miss Grace or Mabel or what-you-please Evans there, they say, No, we have a Miss Ruth Evans."

"And the Franklin Avenue address is listed under George in the phone book. And he's quite right there—a hell of a lot of Evanses. It being a Welsh name and the Welsh being Celts."

"And you're just the little Welshman to know about that," said Rodriguez. "So he hung around the Welfare office, spotted her some way, and followed her home one night."

"Has he got a car?"

"Borrowed one," said Rodriguez impatiently.

"Yes, I want to keep an eye on him and sniff around closer, all right. It could be—it just could be. Come on, let's go back and chase Donaldson down here if he's checked in, and see if D'Arcy's got anything on the practical joker." D'Arcy had got interested in that and begged for some time to check out the sale of the cleanser.

As they came down the corridor from the top of the stairs, Ellis said from the opposite office, "Er—Ivor—would you—"

"Um?" said Maddox, turning.

"Maddox the brain!" said Policewoman Carstairs. "I might have known it'd be you that dreamed up something like this. I might have known. Did you stop to think twice about it? Play like a detective? Oh no, you say off the top of your mind, Just plant Carstairs there!—reliable Carstairs!—all got up like a high-class tart, and wait for the evidence to show. Well, let me tell you—"

"Now, Sue," said Sergeant Daisy Hoffman.

"Look—" began Ellis.

"Did it even once cross your smart detective's mind that—"

Maddox blinked at her. Policewoman Carstairs was mad. She faced him, hands on slender hips, glaring at him. Policewoman Carstairs was, of course, the obvious choice for a plant such as he'd suggested, on Ellis's vice thing. Policewoman Carstairs was twenty-seven, slightly under average height, and had a nice slim figure, crisply curling dark hair, nice blue eyes and a full mouth. She had been a policewoman for six years and had an excellent record: Carstairs was so reliable. She lived with her mother not very far from where Maddox lived, and quite by coincidence they had a Welsh Corgi who bore Maddox's middle name of Goronwy. She also had—he'd always thought—a sense of humor.

"Off the top of his mind, Maddox the brain, he gets this brilliant idea, Just plant Carstairs—"

"Well, hell, Sue, I did say you were the one to plant, the best-looking female we've—"

"And of all the left-handed compliments!" said Policewoman Carstairs dangerously. "So I'm to go to a beauty parlor and get all—all gussied up with the latest crazy new hairdo—and," she swung on Sergeant Hoffman, "if you tell me to get a bleach job, I'm resigning here and now!—and dress up like a —a tart on the make, with the green eye shadow and false eyelashes and the whole bit, and sit around pretending to be a tart with every cop in this precinct—"

"Well, Sue, what the hell, I thought it was a good—"

"Oh, you thought it was a good idea!" said Policewoman Carstairs. She walked up to him and stared him in the eye. "For heaven's sake, Ivor," she said crossly, "it's not that I mind pretending to be— But didn't it just cross your mind that this is a public cocktail lounge? So, fine, I sit there over a drink and ogle the male customers—just the male customers who happen to be cops in this precinct in plain clothes. Fine, fine. Tell them my room number, they come up one by one and we sit around chatting about the weather while the hotel manager gets the impression— So just what am I supposed to do when a real genuine john shows up and starts leering at me? Say, Sorry, I only take every tenth applicant? Use a judo hold on him and give the show away? I'm just asking."

"Oh," said Maddox. "Oh." He hadn't, to tell the truth, thought about that.

"I am," said Policewoman Carstairs, "a reasonably dedicated peace officer, Maddox. I am willing to make all sorts of personal sacrifices for this fine, honorable organization I—fool that I was!—joined and took the oath to. But as a reasonably respectable female—"

"Um," said Maddox. "Take it easy, Sue."

"I'm bound to say I hadn't thought of that," said Ellis. "There'd probably be some, with her acting like that, and—"

"So plant another man there," said Daisy Hoffman calmly. Her eyes twinkled at Sue. "Just use a little more manpower. Different men. If an outsider makes a play for her, the plant muscles in and she makes as if she likes him better. O.K.?"

"Well," said Ellis, "I guess so. As a safeguard. Is that all right with you, Sue?"

"My God," said Policewoman Carstairs, "the things I do for this force! You men can always dream up such nice little games for us! I think any woman is out of her mind to join a police department. Deliberately. Get involved with cops."

Sergeant Daisy Hoffman smiled at her. Sergeant Daisy Hoffman, who was a blonde and still good-looking grandmother, was pretty involved with cops and knew all about that: her husband's name was on the Roll of Honor, cops killed on duty, downtown. Sergeant Daisy Hoffman, like a few other perceptive people at Wilcox Street, was aware that there was one cop Sue Carstairs would dearly love to be involved with—but unlike a lot of other females, Carstairs had the common sense not to let Maddox see that. She looked at Maddox a little curiously: funny about Maddox, he wasn't particularly good looking, only about five nine, none of that overt charm: but somehow, if you were female—even pushing forty-six and a grandmother—there was this something about Maddox. The something that said, the utter male.

"Well, Sue, nobody's ordering you to—"

"If we planted another man there, that'd—"

"Oh, for heaven's sake!" said Policewoman Carstairs. "All right. If you do that." She looked at Maddox bitterly—or,

Sergeant Hoffman thought, tried to. "The *things* I do for—I'd just got a new permanent. And I will *not* have a bleach job."

"There's no law says they've got to be blonde," said Maddox mildly.

"I suppose you should know," said Sue.

Rodriguez, who'd been an interested spectator of this scene, laughed. "Shoe's on the other foot, Sue. They come chasing him. Why, only God knows."

God and females, thought Sergeant Hoffman.

"Oh, all *right!*" said Sue. "As long as you do have another man planted."

The phone was ringing on Maddox's desk as they came into the other office. It was Dennison at the lab.

"Those cigarette butts," he said.

"Yes?" Butts picked up in the disturbed flower bed where, evidently, X had waited for Ruth and Ronnie to show. *Dilly-dilly, come and be killed.*

Ruth and Ronnie. Nice respectable serious young people.

Ritter? A small record of tendency to violence there.

"They're king-size Chesterfields," said Dennison. "Which is about all I can tell you about them. They were smoked in a holder, no chance of running a saliva test."

"Oh, thanks so much," said Maddox.

Ritter the pro heist-man, using a cigarette holder?

Five

THE CIGARETTE HOLDER WENT ON BOTHERING MADDOX LIKE hell. He still thought it was likeliest Ruth had been the target, in connection with her work; in the very nature of things, the people a social worker would deal with would include a higher number of neurotics and unstable people and misfits than a cross-section of the average population. But, a cigarette holder —how many people like Ritter, or Wales, or—

Well, since that report, maybe a lot of unlikely people— Maddox figured, What the hell, himself.

There it was.

Donaldson came in and said, "I found Wales for you. Rather Central did, just now. Some brain down there suddenly remembered we were looking for him and called in. He was in the drunk tank last night, they let him out this morning. I'm just going down to see if he's gone home."

"Let me," said Maddox. Ritter and Wales were his best bets as of right now; he wanted to see Wales himself. "You chase down and help O'Brien lean on some of Ritter's pals. You'll find him somewhere around Ritter's rooming house on San Pedro."

"Oh hell, O'Brien," said Donaldson. "I know the poor guy means well, but isn't he ever going to retire? O.K."

D'Arcy came in looking doleful. "I guess you were right about our joker playing it cute. I've been checking the whole-sale outfits—big warehouses that supply markets and so forth —after a lot of market managers told me they'd be the only places you could buy a gross of gallon bottles at one fell swoop. There are only about a dozen around here—big firms like Smart and Final, you know. I've called four, and got the same answer every time—the managers say they've never, but never, sold an order to any individual like that—except of course the operators of small independent markets that belong to the grocers' association, and they wouldn't be buying by the gross."

"Yes," said Maddox. "It'd take a little time and patience, but he could have gone around and bought it a bottle or so at a time, and got the carton elsewhere."

"Such a hell of a lot of trouble, just—"

Maddox sighed. "Human nature. Suppose we forget the joker. You go see this Frank Gates, will you?"

"They hadn't gone around together lately, I understand. But of course he's got to be talked to. O.K."

Maddox and Rodriguez started off to see if Thomas Wales had gone home.

The Waleses didn't live downtown, but past Boyle Heights nearly into Belvedere, on a narrow shabby street of old frame houses. The street, when Maddox turned into it, looked very dusty and discouraged; there were a lot of shabby-looking children playing up and down the street, this quiet Sun-day afternoon. The street was like a lot of others through-out L.A. County; it was a slum street, and not a slum street. The very word brought to mind the tall dirty tenements, the narrow blacktop canyons between, the laundry fluttering on lines between windows, the kids turned loose on the dirty streets. L.A. didn't have any slums like that, so maybe it could be said not to have real slums at all. But it had a lot of streets like this one, where the small single houses were tumbledown, makeshift places, and most of the bigger single houses had been turned into rooming houses; where nobody could afford the water bill to keep grass green, so it was left brown and patchy in neglected front yards, and nobody bothered repainting or fixing up the houses because most of them were rented. The blacktop of the street was old and rough and pitted, and the sidewalks were cracked; it seemed and probably was a little hotter here than up in Hollywood; the kids seemed a little noisier. There were half a dozen dogs running loose in the street, illegally.

They found the Wales house next to the corner. It was a sad-looking house, a very old little frame house that looked as if it hadn't been constructed very well to start with and had sagged over the years, so that it sat crooked and discouraged on its little plot of ground. One of the panes in one front window was cracked. The house had been painted tan a long while ago, and some of the paint had peeled off. There were steep wooden steps up to a minute front porch, and half of the second riser was missing.

"Why was she coming here in the first place?" asked Maddox as they got out of the car.

"The oldest boy'd been in a little trouble—Grand Theft Auto. Joy riding. First count and he's only fifteen, he got probation. But the family was already on relief and it seemed Ruth had got interested in the girl. Ann Wales. She's got a job—they get a supplemental relief check. Girl apparently trying to hold the family together."

They started up the cracked front walk, and a kid about ten, in the front yard next door with some other kids, said,

"Hey, mister! You better not go there. You sellin' somethin'?"

"Why not?" asked Maddox. The kid looked dirty and ragged, but his eyes were brightly intelligent.

"Because my pop just come home and he's way hung over bad, see, he chased us all out so's he could go to bed. We hadn't even had anything to eat yet either. You wanna wait till Annie comes back, you could talk to her, but she never buys nothing from you guys."

"Well, that's too bad," said Maddox, "but we've got to see your father." They climbed the broken steps and he pushed the bell. They heard its brassy clamor inside the jerry-built house.

"Oh boy, you gonna *catch* it!" said the boy.

When he'd pressed the bell three times and got no answer, Maddox called Wales's name peremptorily. "Come and open up, Wales! Police!"

"Oooh, gee!" moaned all the kids, and started to gather. "What's he done?" "You gonna arrest Tommy's dad?" "What'd he *do*?" Maddox threw them an exasperated glance and tried the door; it was unlocked, and he and Rodriguez went in and shut the door after them.

A man was just coming out of the kitchen, pulling on a pair of pants. "Wales?" said Maddox, and showed him the badge. The man stopped short and showed his teeth.

"Now what'd I do? I swear to God a man can't look crosswise 'thout the goddamn cops— What the hell you want, anyways?"

"Some answers," said Maddox. He felt immediately interested in Wales, even more so than in Ritter, because Wales was afraid. You could read that in every line of him. He wasn't a very prepossessing specimen of humanity at best, and the fear made him less so. He was about fifty, not a big man but gross-looking, with the beer drinker's heavy paunch and pasty, sallow skin that had gone unwashed a lot of his fifty years. Overlong gray hair straggled about his ears, and his eyes were bloodshot, and his face was crisscrossed with the telltale red veins of the drunk. He was wearing a dirty undershirt above stained khaki pants. And at sight of the badge he turned gray with fright. Interesting. He blustered, but was afraid.

"About Ruth Evans," said Maddox.

And that meant something to him, all right. "Who—who's she? I never hearda—"

"You know, all right. You know damn well why we're here, Wales! César, suppose you take a look around for the gun."

"The gun? I ain't got no gun. I never— What the hell you—"

Rodriguez started for the bedrooms. This was a very tired combination living-dining room, no carpet on the floor, miscellaneous pieces of old furniture, not much of it, but it was—unlike the man—quite reasonably clean, and someone had put up a few pictures, arranged some fresh-cut roses in a cheap vase on the mantel. Maddox went over Wales, distastefully; at close quarters, Wales smelled of old sweat, cheap wine, and dirty clothes. He didn't have a gun on him. "So, some answers. Where were you Friday night, Wales?"

Wales breathed heavily and stared at him. "Why? I never hearda—" And the front door opened unexpectedly; Maddox turned.

"Tommy said—the *police*—" said the girl. She'd been shopping; there was a big paper bag of groceries in her arms. "Please, what do you want? Has he—has he done something real bad?"

"Just asking some questions, is it Miss Wales?"

She nodded, putting the bag down on a chair. She could be a pretty girl if she'd troubled to fix herself up, but looking at her, you knew she had so much else to do, to think about, she hadn't the time or energy. She looked about nineteen, brown-haired and brown-eyed; she looked very tired, and the glance she gave her father held contempt and disgust. Her blue cotton housedress was clean and starched, her cheap summer sandals freshly whitened.

"What's he done?"

"We don't know he's done anything, Miss Wales. Just some questions—about Ruth Evans."

"About *Miss Evans?*" She looked bewildered. "But what on earth about? She said she'd come by on Monday—but—"

"Miss Wales," said Maddox, "you didn't know? Miss Evans is dead. Somebody shot her on Friday night. Together with—"

"Sh-shot—" The girl's eyes rolled up whitely and she dropped as suddenly as if she'd been shot herself.

"*Shot her!*" exclaimed Wales in naked horror. Maddox swore and went to the girl, shouting for Rodriguez, who came on the run. They laid her out on the shabby couch. Wales just stood glowering and sweating; you could almost smell his fear, now. The drink wasn't all out of him; he stood swaying, muttering, "Shot—*shot*—"

Maddox found the kitchen: everything needed painting, everything was very old, enamel chipped off the ancient stove and refrigerator, but everything was very clean. Trying to keep a home together for the younger kids, that girl; she was doing a job of it, maybe. And that drunken old bum— And because, probably, she was under age, no way to kick him out and still get the supplemental relief checks to keep the family together.

The rules sometimes didn't allow for individual circumstances.

He took a glass of water back to the living room. Wales had slumped into a chair at the far end of the room from the couch. The girl was sitting up; she thanked him, took the glass. "I'm sorry, Miss Wales. I thought everyone knew. It was in the papers."

"I don't see the papers very often," she said in a thin, tired voice. "It was silly to faint—just the sh-shock—" And then tears began to pour down her face and she groped blindly for a handkerchief. "Miss *Evans*—oh, I just can't bear to think about it—she was so nice, so kind. Just last Friday she was here." She sobbed for several moments, and said chokingly, "I'm sorry, I'm sorry, but she was good to me. She couldn't have been much older than me. You m-mean somebody *murdered* her? Miss *Evans*? Why, she—" Ann Wales stopped short and looked from Rodriguez to Maddox, and sudden fear widened her brown eyes.

"Whoever it was," said Maddox, "waited for her to come home. She'd been out with her fiancé. Whoever it was shot and killed them both, as they sat in the young man's car."

"Oh—my—dear—Lord!" said Ann Wales. "Oh my God." For a moment she looked ready to faint again. She put both hands to her temples and shut her eyes.

The man just sat there slumped over, in the far corner of the room; and you could smell the raw fear on him. Maddox looked at the girl with interest. She was breathing quickly, irregularly.

"Oh no," she whispered. "You coming— I thought at first she'd already— But she said, best I come myself and tell it all just like it was, and then they'd—you'd— She said maybe jail, but anyways— I didn't want to do it, I didn't—my own father —shame the whole family, maybe be in the papers. I never meant tell *her*, but she was so kind. I never had anyone really to talk to before, and—" She looked at them wildly. "You're not telling me *he did it?* He—*killed*—her? Oh no—no—it'd be all my fault." She was sobbing again.

"Please, Miss Wales—please try to control yourself and listen to me," said Maddox. "Miss Evans was coming to see you on Monday? What for? Who were you going to tell what? Please, Miss Wales."

The man sprang up suddenly; both Maddox and Rodriguez were on their feet instantly, ready for trouble. But the man was just shouting, savage and incoherent. "I never—I never did no such thing! Annie, you gotta believe me. You gotta make them know I *never*— Kill somebody—I wouldn't kill nobody. I never I never I never I never—"

"Miss Wales!"

Rodriguez walked over to the man and slapped him hard across the face. Wales collapsed into the chair again and obscenely began to cry, cradling his head in his arms.

"You—you don't know," she said. "You don't know, she didn't— She said there needn't be any—any p-publicity about it. You'd just—take him away. Like that. Oh my God—like my hands were tied—everything left to me, ever since Ma died. And *him. Him.* But what could I *do?* My father—my own father. The other one from the Welfare, last year, I didn't like her—looking down her nose, sort of. What were we supposed to *do?* Ashamed—so ashamed—but I won't be nineteen till next month and that's not of age. I couldn't keep all the kids together if he— I just work part time at Newberrys', and— But Miss Evans said—"

"What was this all about, please, Miss Wales?"

She looked at them with anguished eyes. "I—I see I got to tell," she whispered. "I never meant to tell Miss Evans, but it just come out—she was kind—and she was shocked, I guess, but she said of course it had to come out. And she said, after, she'd speak up for me and try to get a judge let me try to keep us all together, she'd help me get a better job and all—maybe night school."

"After what, Miss Wales?" Something here: something important.

"After—after I'd told, and you'd taken him away. I was afraid—she said she'd go with me, to that big police building, and it'd be all right, she knew one of the officers on the Vice Squad, and—"

The man was still crying. Broken-down old bum.

"What were you going to tell the vice officer?"

She put her hands to her face. It came out in a shamed whisper. "About his—about his—raping Mary. My sister. And trying—me—only I got away from him. It was back when I was fifteen—before Ma died—and she was so sick, the cancer she had. I never told her, but I got a—got a knife and I told him, he ever try it again, I'll stick him, and he knew I meant it too, and he never— And I never *knew* about Mary until—until—" She raised tortured eyes. "What's a person supposed to do, anyways? I had to take what jobs I could get—try earn a little money. I stopped high school after Ma died, I had to, *somebody* had to try earn a little money! Kids got to eat, got to have clothes wear to school, like that. So I wasn't home—and catch *him* holding any kind of job! Had to hide the money I got inside my clothes, he'd have it to buy his drink. Only f-fourteen she was when he— And he said he'd beat her, she told about it, she was scared to tell. Got so she was afraid come home after school, he'd be there, and make the other kids go out, and he'd—" She was sobbing again, but controlled herself determinedly. "And she was scared tell *me*, tell anybody, but he—he hurt her, she tried fight him once when he hurt her and he hit her on the face, and naturally I asked her about it, there was this big mark. And he wasn't there then, that was a couple months back, he was off on a drunk someplace, and she *told* me. So *ashamed*, but what's a person supposed to *do*? I told him, he ever, ever did that to Mary again, I still had my knife, cut his throat. I said, Don't you ever dare go to sleep in this house again, I said—own *father*, but he— But I never meant to tell—tell anybody *outside*, and thank God the other kids never knew. That was another thing, I tell the c-cops, anybody, the younger kids'd get to know— So *ashamed*, but I—"

Maddox looked at Rodriguez. It was, indeed, so much prettier between book covers: the problem posed, the problem neatly solved. People in real life somewhat different. Often, somewhat dirtier: often, somewhat messier: often, you wondered just exactly how far *Homo sapiens* had progressed from the cave with the bones scattered round the fire and Neanderthal squatted grunting over his latest kill. You wondered.

They looked at the man. Something more than a drunken old bum. Neanderthal, suddenly loin-wanting a female and reaching for the handiest one.

"Miss Wales," said Maddox. His eyes looked cold.

"Y-yes?" she said in a muffled voice.

"You told Miss Evans about this, and she was going to come on Monday and take you to see a vice officer, so you could tell him."

"Y-yes. She said—"

"Did your father know about this? Was he here when you told her? That was on Friday?"

She nodded dumbly. "Friday, yes. Along in the afternoon it was. No, my God, he wasn't here, I wouldn't have— But—

but— *Oh my God,* was it him killed her? For *that?* All my fault— I—I was upset-like when we were talking, you can see I'd be upset, can't— No, he wasn't here, of course not, but after—after, when she'd said all that, and we'd arranged it she should come Monday and all, she was so *nice,* she *understood* how it was—after, it was about four o'clock, I went into the kitchen to start the stew and his room's right off there and he was *there,* on the bed, and I didn't know how long— And he looked like he was asleep but I didn't *know*—and—"

"He could have overheard what you were talking about with Miss Evans?" asked Maddox.

Ann Wales nodded. "So *ashamed.* I don't know, but he could have. He could. I don't know—when he came in."

"Did he say anything about it to you? Say he'd heard any of that?"

She shook her head. "But—he wouldn't—maybe—if—oh dear God, don't let it be so! All *my* fault—if he—if he—I mean, if he meant to—"

Maddox looked at Rodriguez. Ruth Evans being nice and understanding, giving the girl time, making that arrangement for Monday. If Wales had overheard all that, he'd have known that nobody but Ruth Evans would know about this sordid little tale until Monday; she'd probably promised the girl not to mention it. And if Ruth Evans should be eliminated, would Ann get up the courage to tell the tale to anybody else very soon?

They looked at Wales, hunched over in the sagging old chair. A drunken bum. Was he capable of that rudimentary planning? Did he know enough to—

"Miss Wales."

"Y-yes."

"Does your father—" my own father—"have a car?"

She nodded. "An old Dodge, yes sir."

So. "Did he know Miss Evans's full name?"

"Yes—why, do you—" She swallowed. "Miss Evans—she asked me to call her Ruth—so nice and kind. I guess he'd hear me saying to Mary or Tommy—but I felt kind of, I don't know, shy about it— She was—"

"Was he home on Friday night?"

She looked up at Maddox. She looked frightened. She looked exhausted. Nine counts against her, still game, still trying. A good girl. "F-Friday? That was— No sir, he wasn't."

"Know what time he came home?"

"No, but it was after I went to sleep, must've been—at ab-about half past twelve. I had Mary's new blouse to finish, I sat up over that, and I went right to sleep after and never heard anything."

Maddox said, "We'll make this as easy on you as we can, Miss Wales." Whose territory were they in here?—the Hollenbeck precinct. "You'll have to come and tell your story now. We'll take him in."

She looked terrified. "Don't be frightened, now," said Rodriguez gently. "You won't be having him around any longer. It'll all be all right." Maddox hoped he was telling her the truth.

She drew a long breath. "All—all right."

Rodriguez went over to Wales, took him by one shoulder, and pulled him up. "Come along, Papa," he said tautly.

So much more genteel between the book covers.

"I—I—I never," said Wales. "I never. Annie, you gotta believe your old dad—"

Six

By the time they booked him in at the County Jail, Wales was in a state of collapse; obviously, he couldn't be questioned immediately. "Tomorrow," said the doctor, to which Maddox returned a few regrettable words.

They got a search warrant, collected D'Arcy, went back, and searched the Wales house from top to bottom. They found a few pornographic paperbacks in the oldest boy's room, and some illicit cosmetics in the ten-year-old girl's room, but they didn't come across the Smith and Wesson 1950 army revolver which had been used on Ruth and Ronnie.

"But he looks very hot for it, doesn't he?" said Rodriguez. "Because it's just the sort of damn-fool thing a fellow like that would do. He couldn't know that between Friday and Monday Ruth might just mention that to somebody—if not her parents, to Ronnie, or somebody at the office—no, he never thinks of that—just, get Ruth out of the way and nobody'll hear about it. Never crossed his mind that then maybe the girl would suspect, and tell us."

"I like him too," agreed Maddox, "but we do need more than just a nice theory. He may come apart when we question him, of course. But let's try to find the gun."

It was six forty-five then. Rodriguez said he had a date and went off. D'Arcy and Maddox went down to the Grotto for dinner. Maddox was feeling better about the case; it looked like breaking fairly soon. He'd had doubts about Ritter; on Wales, only one thing raised a little caution in him, and that was the naked horror in Wales's voice when he'd said, *Shot her?* Had Wales really been that surprised? Overacting? He looked like a hell of a good bet for X.

"Want to come and see this Sandra Bergstrom with me?" he asked D'Arcy. "May as well do a little overtime. Apparently she was one of Ruth's pals at the office—only one there listed in Ruth's address book, at least I take it she's also at the Welfare office, the address is listed as well as her private address. Have to cover everything, and just in case it wasn't Wales— Well, I'm still convinced Ruth was the target, not Ronnie, and it's likeliest the motive was something to do with her work."

"Which I will buy," said D'Arcy. "I see O'Brien and Donny didn't get much." Donaldson had left a note on Maddox's desk.

"Scared a few pals of Ritter's they came across. Not a smell of the gun. So now we go looking hard at Wales's pals, and if they're the same type he is, if any of 'em's keeping the gun for him he ought to break down pretty quick. And it could be too that this is one of those bastards," said Maddox, "where we'll be ninety percent sure who X is and never get enough evidence to charge him. If we can't find the gun—"

"Yeah," said D'Arcy. This whole case—Ritter, Wales, somebody unknown, whoever—might hang on the gun. No charge on anybody was going to stand up unless they could tie the charged man tight to that gun; and either Ritter or

Wales or anybody else could have thrown it in the nearest storm drain or buried it in an empty lot. Where did you start to look But of course anybody—especially a Ritter or a Wales —might be a little chary of throwing away anything that valuable, so—

They paid their checks and drove up to St. Andrews Place. It was an old apartment house but well maintained: probably larger, more comfortable apartments than some of the new cramped ones. They climbed carpeted stairs and hunted for apartment 12; Maddox pushed the bell. After a while he pushed it again.

The peephole in the door opened and one large blue eye regarded them through it. "Yes?"

"Miss Bergstrom? We're police officers, we'd like to—" Maddox held up his badge as identification.

"Oh damn! I was coming to see you tomorrow, and all fixed up too, because I've never met any cops and I— And now you have to catch me like this! I've just washed my hair. Oh damn, I suppose I've got to let you in. How maddening. It's about Ruth, isn't it? Just a minute." A bolt was pulled back, a chain unfastened. The door swung open.

Miss Bergstrom had an attractive voice, husky and young-sounding. When the door opened they saw that she was young, probably younger than Ruth Evans. She was a bouncy little blonde with an eye-catching figure clad in brief white shorts and a blue halter bra, and her legs were eye-catching too. She had very blue eyes and a good deal of natural flaxen-blond hair, which she was drying vigorously with a towel. The damp hair was rapidly springing into natural ringlets.

"Well, come in, come in. Damn," she said mournfully, "to think you have to catch me like this, when I was going to wear my new navy and maybe a hat."

— 64

Maddox suppressed a grin. She'd have made a much bigger impression dressed as she was. "Just a few questions, if you don't mind."

"Sit down, sit down," she said, staring at them with frank curiosity. "What're your names?"

Maddox told her. He sat down on the couch. It was a bright, welcoming room, some modern reproductions on the walls, a few pieces of good Danish-styled furniture. Sandra Bergstrom said interestedly, "Is he deaf?"

Maddox looked at D'Arcy and sighed. D'Arcy was standing transfixed, staring at Miss Bergstrom bemusedly. "D'Arcy!" he said loudly. The inevitable had happened; D'Arcy had fallen in love again. Well, a little excuse maybe.

"What?" said D'Arcy absently.

"Sit down," said Maddox. "Don't mind him, Miss Bergstrom, he's—um—got a lot on his mind. Now, you knew Ruth—"

"Oh yes. It's an awful thing to've happened, I was terribly shocked when I saw the paper, but it's not as if we'd been close friends or anything. I'm one of the stenos in the office, not a social worker. Thank you, no. I have enough trouble managing my own life without taking on other people's." Still briskly toweling her hair, she divided a grin between them, three quarters of it at Maddox. Naturally. "But I might know something about it, reason I was coming to see you. You haven't found whoever did it yet?"

"Well, we're not sure—still checking," said Maddox vaguely. "What do you have to tell us?" Something new? Something else?

"Well—you can smoke if you like, I'll have one myself in a minute, when my hair—you *would* walk in when I look like this! Damn curly hair, you never can do a thing with it."

She put the towel across her lap and reached to the coffee table for a cigarette. D'Arcy lunged eagerly to light it for her and nearly set her halter on fire. "Hey!" she said. "Take it easy! Well, I don't know if she'd mentioned it to anybody else. She was an awfully *serious* girl, you know—sort of dedicated. That kind. My heavens above, who likes their work all the time, doesn't do some cussing about it once in a while? Even cops, I guess. Excuse me, I suppose you don't like being called cops." She smiled at them: she looked like a pert junior-high miss, all very excited about helping out the Good Guys.

"Well—" said Maddox. "I guess especially cops feel that way sometimes. Why not?"

"Well, she didn't, I mean. She was all so earnest and dedicated she— It was as if she felt sort of guilty if she got fed up with the job sometimes, if you know what I mean. I said I didn't know her very well, and I didn't, but I can size people up, you know. And that's how she was. Which is what sort of makes me think she wouldn't have mentioned this to any of the other social workers. We just happened to be in the ladies' room at the same time—this was last Thursday. And I don't know if it means anything at all," said Sandra earnestly, "but we got talking a little and she told me she was getting to hate going to see this one family she had on her list—it was a Mexican name, Reyes I think—or Alvarez—because of the landlord where they lived. She said she was really a little afraid of him."

"Why, did she say?"

"Oh yes—he was making the most lurid passes at her!" The blue eyes opened wider. "Honestly! She said he'd lie in wait for her on the stairs, and one time he grabbed her and tried to drag her into his apartment, but she managed to get away from him. The way she described him, I think he must be a little nutty—the kind who thinks he's irresistible. And lately, she said, since the time he grabbed her, he'd threatened her. Because she didn't think he was irresistible. I don't know if it means anything."

D'Arcy came to life, beaming at her fondly, and said, "Why didn't she complain to the car on the beat?"

Sandra said instantly, "I think she was a bit ashamed to tell about it." She made a little grimace. "Good trained social workers are supposed to be able to cope efficiently with any problem—you know the bit. And she did think she was good."

"Oh. Nose in the air?" asked Maddox.

"Not really, no. I guess she was good. No, no, she wasn't like that, she was friendly. But serious."

"Well. This is a little surprise, Miss Bergstrom. Did you know that your name was in her address book and both the office address and this one listed? We'd figured you were one of her friends down there, another—"

"Oh," said Sandra. "But why on earth— Say, I'll bet I know why, at that. She was efficient, the way I said. No, we weren't specially friendly, but now I recall, I did happen to mention to her once—this wasn't so long ago, maybe a couple of weeks —that my sister Nadine's engaged to marry a lawyer—that is, he's not yet but he'll graduate next year, and he'd been talking about finding somebody to share an office with him. And her boy friend was a law student too, wasn't he? Could be she figured maybe they'd get together, if her fiancé wanted to, I could introduce—"

"Probably. This amorous landlord. Did she tell you his name?"

"I don't think she knew it herself. She did say he's Italian.

I guess it was. And the family she went to see there—yes, I'm sure it was Reyes."

"Well, another something," said Maddox dubiously. He still liked Wales. "Thanks very much." He got up.

"Oh, you have to go?" She was disappointed. "Do you want me to come in and make a statement or something? I'd be glad—"

"Well, not until we know a little more about it, thanks. He may not have anything to do with it."

She trailed them to the door, looking wistful. "Just an awful thing to happen. I should think it must have been a lunatic—like that landlord, you know. I just can't imagine anybody having any real reason to murder somebody like Ruth Evans, for heaven's sake. Of course, I suppose whoever it was could have wanted to kill her fiancé instead. He was good looking, wasn't he? But he looked awfully serious too."

D'Arcy cleared his throat and said, "Ah—when we do find out about it, I—maybe you'd like to hear all the details?"

"Oh, that'd be interesting," she said, looking at Maddox. Naturally. He'd never know why.

Poor D'Arcy.

Maddox listened to a rapt account of Miss Bergstrom's charms all the way back to the Grotto's parking lot, where D'Arcy had left his car.

He went home to the little house on Gregory Avenue and tried to settle down with a book, but the case kept sliding into his mind. He thought afterward he must have had something like a premonition, because at that time the case was looking not too bad at all.

Wales looked very good as chief suspect, and there was

every possibility that tomorrow, when they got down to questioning him seriously, he'd come apart and tell them all about how he'd shot Ruth Evans, followed her home and maybe seen her leave on her date with Ronnie—maybe parked along Franklin in his old Dodge—so he'd got a gun, or already had one, and waited there for them to come home. And tell them what he'd done with the gun too, so, a nice tight charge.

And if it wasn't Wales, it could easily have been Ritter. Haul him in for some questioning in depth, eventually he might break.

Or it could even have been Miss Bergstrom's amorous landlord. You just never knew how people would react to this or that.

The cigarette holder continued to bother him a little. Not many people used cigarette holders. But there was no absolute guarantee that those cigarette butts had been dropped by whoever shot Ruth and Ronnie.

D'Arcy had found Frank Gates, her former boy friend, this afternoon. Gates looked perfectly open and clear. He hadn't seen Ruth in at least six months, he said. There'd never been anything serious between them; they'd dated each other some, more of propinquity than anything else; he'd been sorry and shocked to read about how she'd been murdered, but— And last Friday night he'd been with five friends, all male, at a poker session. Names readily given: not checked out yet, but probably they would. Alibi.

What the hell did her former boy friends have to do with it?

It was almost certainly Wales. The drunk, the bum, the lecher. Where had he got the gun? More important, Maddox thought all of a sudden, where had he got the money to get the gun? He could have borrowed it—he could have stolen it.

It probably wouldn't take much questioning in depth to break down Thomas Wales.

The inquest was scheduled for tomorrow. Also, George Ellis was setting up Sue as a plant at that hotel tomorrow. Maddox wondered a little sleepily how Sue would do at that—wondered how she'd look, all fixed up as the obvious high-class tart. He smiled. Nice girl, Carstairs. Good policewoman.

That practical joker. If nothing else important came up, once they'd cleared up the Ruth and Ronnie thing, he supposed they ought to make some effort to find the practical joker. Malicious mischief.

People with that kind of mind—the infinite trouble they'd go to, just for the little joke—

The sight of that gross pink pig came back to him suddenly and he began to laugh. Well, damn funny in a way, of course—

And the gross of cleanser and the works of Freud for the fanatic housekeeper.

He wondered if they'd have any more practical jokes. Probably. Once one like that got started—

He had just a faint glimmer, just then, about that: that they weren't only practical jokes. That the joker wasn't just picking out the little personal foibles to make fun of, but maybe—maybe trying to accomplish something?

Like that?

The pink pig, to say gently to Clyde Endler, Look, friend, you've been pouring it down kind of heavy, maybe you better stop and think.

The cleanser and the Freud, to say with a grin to Mrs. Foster, Look, lady, you know what they say about your kind, let's not carry it too far.

Well.

Suppose they didn't break Wales down and never got any

more on him? One of those things. Thinking of Wales, Maddox grimaced and went out to the kitchen to build himself a drink. It wasn't the first time he'd run into one like Wales: but they always made you wonder.

The do-good people living nice respectable normal lives didn't quite believe in the Waleses: made shocked and horrified noises when they read about them in the *Times*. Any cop had run across the Waleses and worse, often enough that he got to feeling a little cynical about the righteous do-good people.

Another headline in the *Herald* tonight, Defense Lawyer Charges Improper Police Procedure.

The do-good people who hadn't any conception of the dirt every cop had to deal with, get to know intimately, the incredible dirt at the bottom of things—eternal Neanderthal—so the do-good people could go on living nice normal lives, safe and unmolested.

Oh, maybe more than other people cops got fed up with the job. The thankless job.

The phone rang and he picked it up, coming back into the living room with his highball. "Maddox."

"Oh, Ivor. Sally, darling. Look, your day off this month is Tuesday, isn't it?—oh, I'm a smart girl, I remember things like that!" Sally Scott chuckled seductively. Well, you could say a very seductive female, Sally. "So you can come to my cocktail party. . . . Now, Ivor! Just a few people I know, and they'll all be off by six thirty or seven, so you can come late—six-ish—and stay on for dinner afterward. . . . You can too. It's a good two weeks since I've seen you."

"Well," said Maddox. Quite a girl, Sally—

"Steaks," said Sally, her husky voice sliding down the register intimately. "Afterward. Hmm?"

"Um," said Maddox. "I don't drink cocktails, woman. I don't like silly parties with a lot of idiotic chatter about the latest TV programs."

"Six fifteen," said Sally. "And I'll chase everybody out by at least seven. That's a promise, darling."

"No actors?" said Maddox. You never knew who you'd run into at Sally's parties.

"Cross my heart, lover man."

"Well—six fifteen," said Maddox. "See you."

He rather liked Sally Scott. An honest wench. Didn't pretend to be anything but what she was.

Tuesday—

He got to the office at ten to eight on Monday morning. There was this and that to get done today, and so it was all the more annoying when they got the call, at eight o'clock— again from Stoner in his patrol car—about the latest practical joke.

This one a bit more serious.

Fortunately, Mr. William Sherriss, who owned and operated a dry-cleaning shop next to the shop owned by Mr. Martin Rasmussen, had been parking his car in the alley behind the block of shops on La Brea Avenue just as Mr. Rasmussen was unlocking the rear door of his place, which was an electric appliance and service store. Otherwise, Mr. Rasmussen might —Sherriss said to Stoner, shocked—have lain there undiscovered for hours.

Somebody—the practical joker, ten to one and no takers— had got into Rasmussen's shop overnight and, of all things, set up a booby trap. Rather cleverly, over the back door of his shop. All the shop owners along there parked in the rear alley and would normally enter their shops by the back doors.

The practical joker had, with some ingenuity, so arranged a large cardboard carton, with a system of ropes and a pulley, that when the rear door was opened the carton would be up-ended to discharge its contents onto whoever was coming in.

The carton had been filled with a numerous miscellaneous collection of children's toys, and among them was a good-sized toy fire engine, a pretend flame thrower, and a model of a Ford truck, any of which—being discharged from ten feet above the victim's head—could have done the damage.

At any rate, Mr. Sherriss had heard the clatter as the contents of the carton fell, and gone to look, and discovered Rasmussen unconscious on the floor there.

With a concussion, as it developed.

Rasmussen was still unconscious in Hollywood Hospital.

And this time their practical joker had maybe pulled a felony. Assault. If in a funny kind of way.

And just why?

The same joker responsible for the pig, the gross of cleanser? It looked that way, because—

"Children's toys," said Rodriguez. "Now what the hell?" He stood and looked at the clutter in the back room of Rasmussen's shop. Toy trucks, a skate board, jigsaw puzzles, stuffed animals, crayons, an Erector set— "What the hell?"

"On top of everything else!" said Maddox angrily. "The goddamned practical joker! I don't suppose he intended the man to be actually hurt, but there it is—he was. So we have to go looking. On a felony, now. Damn it."

"But why the toys?" asked Rodriguez.

"How the hell should I know? And damn it, that inquest— And we've got to question Wales—"

Seven

THEY HAD TO START WORK ON IT, AS IMPOSSIBLE AS IT LOOKED.
Now it was a more serious charge.

The inquest was scheduled for ten o'clock. Maddox said,
"And just maybe the longer we let Wales stew, the easier
he'll come apart. O.K., let's do what we can here." He called
back to Wilcox Street and asked for Dabney. "A hell of a
job, but he's going to dust all these damn toys, and the carton.
And then, just on the long chance, he's going to chase up to
the Fosters' and dust that carton and all those damn bottles.
The routine does pay off. And you and I are going to see Rasmussen's wife. Shouldn't take long. Then the inquest, and
we'll let Wales go until after lunch."

When Dabney got there, heard about his job and groaned,
they started for Rasmussen's home address. The hospital said
his condition wasn't serious, he'd probably be released tomorrow—just a little concussion.

The Rasmussens lived on Greenacre Avenue. "About five
blocks from Detroit," said Maddox thoughtfully. "About ten
blocks from Higman. Roughly the same neighborhood. Area,
anyway. But somebody who knows both the Endlers and the
Fosters, who don't know each other. Odd."

Rodriguez grunted. He had pulled the latest *Saint Mystery Magazine* from his pocket; but the practical joker, as the offbeat thing, had captured his imagination and after a minute he put the magazine down and said, "Something else funny. The joker knowing about these—er—personality quirks. That's what the first two were aimed at. Probably, when we find out, this one too. So how come? I mean, you can't just say somebody who knows that area, or even people in that area. Such as—as a Helms Bakery truck driver, or the milkman. Because how would people like that know about Endler's drinking or Mrs. Foster's fanatical cleanliness?"

"Yes," said Maddox. "Odd is no word for it."

The house on Greenacre Avenue was a nice little house, part frame and part stucco, with the inhumanly neat flower beds and edged lawn that bespoke an enthusiastic gardener. But there was a tricycle on the little front porch, and from inside the open screen door came excited children's voices, the blare of a TV. Maddox and Rodriguez stared at the tricycle. "We're damn fools," said Maddox, "she'll be at the hospital."

But she wasn't. She came to the door looking distracted, a dark young woman, pretty in a quiet way, smoothing her hair nervously; she was neatly dressed and made up. "I'm sorry, I can't possibly listen to anybody selling— My husband— Marty, be quiet! I'm very busy, I— Oh. Oh, you're police officers? About Martin? Oh yes. Such a morning I've had, right in the middle of the breakfast dishes, they called about Martin and I had to get Betty Field from next door to stay with the children and rush right over to the hospital, and I thought the cab would never come, my car's in the garage. He's perfectly all right, you know—just a bang on the head—but he's going to be furious. Absolutely furious. Men do make such a fuss over things. Well, it wasn't at all a nice thing to do—all those toys—" She stopped, looking oddly both angry and pleased. By this time they were all in the living room; it was furnished in Early American, and the upper half of it, as it were, was neat, while the floor was littered with nursery-age picture books, toys, and stuffed animals in various stages of dilapidation. Two children sprawled on the floor raptly watching a cartoon on TV. The volume was deafening.

Mrs. Rasmussen went over and snapped it off. "You two go outside and play now. I've got to talk to—" Instant wails arose. The boy was about five, the girl about three. "And *look* at this mess! No, you can't see the cartoon. Outside, I said! Please, Marty, do be a good boy now. Mother's having a terrible day and if you'd just try to help a little— Take care of Peggy, now—"

It took her about five minutes to get them out. She asked Maddox and Rodriguez to sit down, sat down herself, and said rather breathlessly, "They can be such nuisances, can't they? I mean, I wouldn't be without them, but there's no denying it's difficult. I mean, you can't expect children to be—to be anything but children, can you?" She looked at them anxiously. "Of course, it was someone who knew about that, I saw that at once, when that nice policeman explained what had happened. I'm afraid—once I knew Martin was all right— I did think it was rather funny. Amusing, I mean."

"What, Mrs. Rasmussen?" asked Maddox.

"Why, the joke. I don't suppose whoever did it meant to really hurt Martin—it was just to, maybe, make him stop and think a little. Don't you think? Because Martin certainly isn't mean or cruel in any way—he just doesn't stop to *think*. If you know what I mean."

"Mrs. Rasmussen—just what do you mean?"

"This—whoever did it. Set the booby trap." She smiled. "If I didn't know better I'd think it could have been Mrs. Faulkner—she gets quite indignant about how Martin behaves—she baby-sits for us quite a lot, she's raised seven of her own and has nine grandchildren, imagine—but of course she wouldn't know how and anyway her arthritis— Well, I knew *that* right away, that it's somebody who knows Martin. You see, Martin's almost twelve years older than I am, he was thirty-seven when we were married, and he doesn't mean to be impatient or—you know—but he's just never been around small children. And, well, children will be children, won't they? They will forget about not running across his flower beds, and I have to keep at them about leaving their things on the front lawn. Martin has a fit—and naturally when he comes home he wants to relax, but there are these TV programs they like to see just before dinner, and he gets very cross about not being able to read the paper in peace."

"I see," said Maddox. So, the practical joker knew Rasmussen's foibles too. And so the mystery of the children's toys was explained.

"I've tried to talk to him," she said a little wistfully. "Sometimes he really tries, I know, and then some little thing will set him off again. I don't want them to grow up afraid of their father, but you can see—"

"Yes," said Maddox. The joker this time, with his booby trap of toys, saying to Rasmussen, Look, friend, this situation can boomerang on you: you stop and think, children are a long-range project, not just today's upsets or pleasures. "Can you think of anybody you know who'd be likely to do such a thing?"

"I simply can't imagine," said Mrs. Rasmussen, shaking her head. "Nobody we know ever plays practical jokes. I can't think of a soul."

"Except Mrs. Faulkner."

"Oh, but it couldn't be her. She's seventy-two and quite lame."

Maddox tried to conceive of Mrs. Faulkner decorating the pink pig and manhandling that carton of bottles, and failed. "Do you know anyone named Endler?"

"Why, no, we don't."

"Or Foster?"

"We know some Fosters in Long Beach."

"Well," said Maddox. "Thanks very much anyway."

"Now who, doing what in the normal course of the day's work, would get to know all these personal things about people who don't know each other?" wondered Rodriguez, outside.

"I'm like Mrs. Rasmussen," said Maddox. "I simply can't imagine."

The inquest was purely formal—held jointly on both bodies —and ended with an open verdict. The coroner took full evidence, so that brought them up to noon. Maddox, Rodriguez, D'Arcy, and Ellis went to the Grotto for lunch and then, fortified, drove down to the County Jail to question Wales.

Wales was a sorry-looking object when the bailiff brought him into the interrogation room. The liquor was out of him now, and he was a gross, dirty, unkempt man, old beyond his years, full of sniveling self-pity and fright and desperation.

He started right in, before anyone asked him anything, "I never did it. I never done no murder. You can't pin that on me. I never—"

"Sit down, Wales," said Maddox. Wales shuffled up to the straight chair and sat, looking fearfully up at them grouped loosely around him, professional men about to do a very routine professional job. "Where were you on Friday night, Wales?"

"I—I—was with some friends o' mine. Some friends. I never—"

"Which friends?" asked Rodriguez, bringing out his notebook.

"Oh. I gotta think. I gotta—uh—Al Dugan was one. And—and Jimmy Russell. And I guess Bob was with us awhile—you gotta believe me I never, I never— Huh? Bob—Bob Cheevers. Yeah, that's right."

"Where?" asked D'Arcy.

Wales kept turning his head from one to the other as they asked their questions.

"Uh—Friday—uh—a bar down Third, I guess named Tony's."

"When?" asked Ellis. "What time?"

"Uh—I guess we went there about eight o'clock. I—"

"But you were home on Friday afternoon," said Maddox.

Wales blinked at him. "Yeah. Yeah, I—"

"You came in the back door and you heard your daughter Ann talking to the social worker. Ruth Evans. You heard her—"

"No, I didn't, I never knew that woman, I—"

"—heard her telling Ruth Evans all about how you were sleeping with your own daughter Mary. And had tried to rape Ann once. And you knew—"

"No, I never—"

"You bastard," said D'Arcy dispassionately, "you did! You

knew you could get a nice jail sentence if that came out to a vice cop, and you—"

"No, please, you gotta— I never—"

"Where'd you get the gun, Wales?"

"When did you get the gun? Before you went to the bar?"

"You followed Ruth back to her office? Or did you just go there and wait for her to come out, so you could follow her home?"

"I— Jesus, you got me all confused. I never *had* no gun, I didn't—"

"How long were you at the bar with your pals?"

"Jeez, I dunno. I dunno. Maybe they could tell you— but I—"

"Come on, come on, you left under your own steam? You weren't drunk?" asked Maddox.

"No, I wasn't drunk, I hadn't but about two bucks on me, I was drinkin' beer. I didn't take no notice o' the time, maybe it was like ten o'clock."

"Did you have the gun on you then?" Ellis.

"I never had no—"

"Where did you get it?" D'Arcy.

"I didn't—"

"Did you have your car out that night?" Rodriguez.

"Yeah, yeah, I had the car. I wasn't drunk, and I never had no—"

"You heard your daughter telling all that to Ruth Evans, didn't you? You heard her say she'd tell a vice officer on Monday. And you were scared, weren't you, Wales? You knew what that would mean—jail. But if you could get to the Evans woman before—"

"No, I didn't." Wales started to cry. "You gotta believe me."

It went on like that for quite some time. It was boring, it was frustrating, it was necessary. They were patient with him; they gave him glasses of water and cigarettes; they kept asking the same questions over and over, and sometimes Wales cried and sometimes he just stared at the floor; but he was breaking down. They got more or less definite answers from him about where he said he'd been Friday night; he admitted he hadn't got home until about two A.M. He was shaking now, and he looked very tired and old and broken, and it was the casual question from D'Arcy that ended it at last.

"About two o'clock?" said D'Arcy, and bent to stare at him. "And did you make love to your *daughter* that night, Wales?"

"For Christ's sake, leave me alone!" screamed Wales suddenly. He leaned forward in the chair, clasping his hands tight over his ears. "All right all right I tell you—I took her I did it to her she was fourteen pretty and young I was maybe a little drunk but my wife she was sick never no good for loving like that anyways no good no good and I— I tell you all right I did that and you put me in jail for it. She was there and I maybe was drunk but I—but I— It was like pay back her ma because she didn't like it either she was scared and said I hurt her and her damn ma such a hell a refined lady what the goddamned hell she think getting married's all *about*—and she— and she—all right I tell you that but you can't make me say about killing because I never I never I never— I heard her all right I heard her tell—Annie—then—about going see—vice cop —but I never— I went and got drunk because I was scared you put me in jail—and why the hell I ever got on the drink start with—the priest says—refined holy as hell lady— I tell you that but you can't say about a gun because I never I never I never and inna million years I ain't gonna—"

And then he passed out cold and fell onto the floor, so that was the end of that session.

"What do you think?" said Ellis tiredly on the steps outside.

"I don't know," said Maddox. "Damn it, it's this way and that way, George. Isn't it? That's a nice little motive. But we don't have to show motive, that says nothing really, because we both know a lot of homicides get committed for no sensible motive at all. But if Wales is X, I am just a little surprised that he didn't break. Considering his type. No will power, no pride, no guts. That kind usually come apart without much trouble, don't they?"

"They do," said Ellis. He put on his hat, a big sandy nondescript man there beside Maddox, and then took it off to scratch his head. "So maybe he isn't the X on Ruth and Ronnie? What about that Ritter?"

Maddox shrugged. "Look at him again closer. Maybe." He looked at his cigarette. "I'd like to get this bird. When you think about all the worthless punk kids—and then two like Ruth and Ronnie. The earnest, dedicated young people."

"Yeah," said Ellis.

"She's got these great big blue eyes," D'Arcy was rhapsodizing to Rodriguez, "and this figure— I tell you, boy, the minute I saw her— And how the hell could I ever tell her what my name—" Poor D'Arcy. Anybody who called him by his first name was asking for a punch in the jaw. And if he wasn't quite so susceptible—

They went back to Wilcox Street. Carter was on the desk, and when he saw Ellis beckoned him over. Ellis came upstairs a few minutes later looking harassed.

"Ivor, will you fill in a little? That plant. Sue's due to go into her act again at four, and I had a uniformed man—Connally—detailed to stand by as the safeguard, butt in, in case somebody except our boys approaches her, and now for God's sake—he was on regular tour in a car, of course—he's got this freeway tangle, five cars involved, and he can't—"

"Oh hell," said Maddox, who wanted to sit and do some brooding on Wales. "All right." He looked at his watch; it was ten to four. "What's the address?" And it had been his idea, but he didn't even know that. Ellis gave it to him.

He went downstairs again and drove out to Fairfax Avenue. It was a classier place than he'd expected, the Golden Cock, with a restaurant occupying the ground floor, cocktail lounge attached—Cleveland-the-pimp's hotel. At this time of day, in the nature of things, Ivor Maddox was in need of a shave, and his suit had come off the sixty-buck rack five years ago; he hoped they'd let him in. But nobody challenged him. He got a Scotch and water at the bar and carried it to a small table at the rear of the room. It was a long narrow room, not too dark because a wide archway at the right side led into the dining room. It was decorated in very modernistic style, black and gold; the wallpaper was printed with stylized gold roosters. Not too many customers at this hour: a morose man huddled on a bar stool, a middle-aged couple handsomely dressed, animatedly talking, at another of the small tables, two sedate-looking men at a third, drinking Bloody Marys. And, of course, Sue.

Policewoman Carstairs.

He'd been a few minutes late, and for half a second there she'd looked terribly relieved to see him.

He couldn't say he blamed her. High-class tart be damned, he thought, Main Street was more like it. She looked, he thought, like hell. Her dark hair was piled on top of her head to towering height, stiffly lacquered, with long wispy bangs covering her brows, and she had on a lot of make-up, too much green eye shadow and mascara, and that new pale lipstick in a mauve-pink color; and she had on a black taffeta sheath dress with no sleeves, cut impossibly low for the nice cleavage effect, and clocked sheer black nylons and a pair of gold mules with four-inch heels. She had on long dangly jade-green earrings, an armful of gold bangles, and a jade-green cigarette holder, and she looked absolutely like hell, thought a shocked Maddox—nice reliable Carstairs, the efficient policewoman, and it *had* been his idea, but—

He was aware that this was not her first performance—call it that. She'd started out here (having registered this morning) according to schedule, about one o'clock; and the first plain-clothes man to make the flagrant assignation, and casually leave ten minutes after her to go up to her room, had been a wire-tap expert borrowed from Central. He'd gone over her room here for a tap, and evidently found none, since the plan was still in operation.

My God, thought Maddox, feeling slightly outraged for no reason, she looks like *hell*. All that eye shadow—and the damn cigarette holder—

A cigraette holder. Wales? Well, nothing said those butts belonged to X. . . .

He sat, nursing his drink, and (still feeling absurdly shocked, the nice girl Carstairs was) watched Sue unobtrusively. He knew that around five o'clock Brougham was due to come in —one of the Wilcox Street detectives—and pick her up, make the obvious date, and subsequently pussyfoot up to her room; it was to be hoped, observed and reported on to Cleveland.

But about a quarter to five, before Brougham showed, the eventuality Sue had foreseen arose: the genuine amorous john, naturally attracted by the sheath (for some reason Maddox felt a little uneasy to notice what a hell of a good figure she had), the eye shadow, and the generally available look. The fellow at the bar. She'd taken another bar stool, and he'd been watching her interestedly, finally moved down next to her.

Maddox waited to see if she could shake him herself, but the man was persistent—half drunk or more. She parried him, laughing, fended him off when he tried to kiss her. Maddox got up and carried his drink to the bar.

"Hey, you quit annoyin' this lady, mister."

"Who's annoyin'—"

"You are. On your way, bum." He gave the man a shove.

"Hey, who you pushin' around, hey, look." But he was a smaller man than Maddox, and quite drunk. He took a couple of steps back, hesitated, gave a weak smile, and stumbled toward the door.

Play it out, now.

"Gee, thanks," said Sue, fluttering her false eyelashes at Maddox. The bartender was being an interested witness. "These drunks."

"No respect for a lady," said Maddox, leering at her.

"That's right. My name's Sally, what's yours?"

Sally Scott, tomorrow. My God, that dress: who'd picked it out? She looked like absolute hell. "Johnny. You're kind of cute, Sally."

They leaned heads together, whispering. The barkeep watched from a little way off. She had on a lot of heady, musky perfume: and he'd had only the one drink, but it made his head swim a little.

The barkeep was looking the other way, listening hard.

"Room three twelve," she whispered, and slid off the bar stool. "Well, nice meeting you, Johnny. See you around maybe."

"Sure," said Maddox. He didn't turn to watch her hip-sway out. He said to the bartender, "Another shot, hey?" and when it came, he added it to his highball, drank it off fast, paid and went out. The bartender would, he hoped, be sliding over to the dining-room door to give the high sign to a waiter or bellhop.

Feeling obscurely angry, he went into the lobby proper of the hotel, walked to the self-service elevator, and rode up to the third floor. Someone (he hoped) would be noticing.

Sue let him into Room three twelve. It was a nice room, good-sized, with a beige-covered double bed, a mahogany dresser, and a couple of upholstered chairs.

"You," said Maddox frankly, "look like hell. Sadie Thompson."

"Well, it was your idea," said Policewoman Carstairs. "Thanks very much for the rescue."

"Don't mention it. You and Brougham'll have to put off your—um—assignation a little bit, after this ostensible session with me."

"I suppose," said Sue. She sat down in the other chair.

"You don't approve of the getup? I thought it was quite authentic." She touched her hair. "Very latest thing."

"Too damned authentic," said Maddox. He realized that some of his feeling was outrage that a nice girl like Carstairs should have to play such a part, get herself up like this, in the hope of trapping a pro procurer-pimp like this goddamned worthless Cleveland—mostly on account of that unrealistic State Supreme Court decision on resorting. Well, she was a cop too. Cops let themselves in for things.

He lit a cigarette. He felt rather uneasily aware of that damn obtrusive double bed. "How's the pup?" he asked.

"Oh, fine, thanks. Got clawed by Mrs. Howard's cat the other day."

"He ought to know better."

She was fiddling with the cigarette holder. A *cigarette holder*. He looked at his watch. Give it till six. Let Brougham wait.

Wales? Funny a type like that hadn't broken right away.

The joker. The children's toys.

"Sue," he said.

"Well?"

"This damn practical joker thing. It's somebody—got to be somebody—who knows all these people. Knows their—um—personal foibles. To some extent, at least. But they don't know each other—no connection. And you know, say it's a—a territory of some kind—Helms Bakery route, milkman, Fuller Brush man—people like that wouldn't have any chance to get to know— I don't see it. I don't see how the hell—" And damn it, he wasn't an adolescent, they were two cops doing a job together, but—

"Oh?" said Sue. She considered. "I see what you mean.

César told me something about it. Funny." She drifted over to the dresser and looking at herself critically patted her hair. "No, none of those. But I had a little thought. What about a TV repairman?"

"What?" said Maddox. "What?"

"A TV repair service. Those men—coming into houses, you know, sometimes there for quite some time, and nobody paying them much attention—"

"For God's *sake!*" said Maddox, awed.

Eight

HE LEFT THE HOTEL AT SIX, NOT GLANCING INTO THE BAR, aware that Brougham would be sitting there wondering where the devil Sue was, and Connally or another man sitting in as the safeguard. He was so impressed with Sue's little idea that he went straight back to the office and called the Endlers. Did they have a TV? Certainly they had. Did they usually call the same place when it needed adjustment or repairs? Yes, it was a Packard-Bell and the plant being right here they always called the Packard-Bell Service, but what were the police—

Maddox thanked Endler and tried the Fosters. Yes, sure they had a TV. Well, they carried repair-and-parts insurance on it, the Packard-Bell plant being right here you could do that on that make, so when anything went wrong they'd just call Packard-Bell Service. And why the hell were the police interested?

Maddox felt a little excited. Packard-Bell. Had he found the link? Coincidences did happen, but— He called the Rasmussen house and got Mrs. Rasmussen. She told him her husband would be out of the hospital tomorrow, he was perfectly all right. "But he seemed a little quiet. I thought he'd be furious, but he's— I wonder if he has been doing some thinking.

Excuse me? Our TV? Why on earth— Well, yes, we do always have the same people, though I don't see why— Oh well, it's a Packard-Bell and we carry their private insurance on it, it's really very worth while, you never have to pay for parts or labor and we've already had two new picture tubes without any charge at all."

"Thank you very much," said Maddox fervently. The first link he'd found connecting all three people who'd suffered the practical jokes. Quite an idea Sue had had, all right. And in a way he could see it, the TV repairman often in the house for an hour or more, and still the life of the house going on around him. Of course, with a stranger present, Mrs. Endler wouldn't be apt to start a fight with Endler about his drinking, but the man could have overheard a few words from another room: probably Mrs. Foster's house (and he might have been there while she was doing her housework) would tell the story there; and he could have overheard things at the Rasmussens' too ("now don't leave your tricycle there, you know how it annoys Daddy"—or Mrs. Rasmussen talking with a friend about that). All right. This was the first possibility they'd come across.

But the practical joker and a doubtlessly busy TV serviceman? Of course people did come all sorts, and you never knew who'd do what. But the practical joker, with his rather impish sense of humor, the infinite trouble he'd gone to over his little jokes—

Well, it was a possibility.

He hadn't really anything he wanted to do on his day off, reflected Maddox, until, of course, he was due at Sally's at six fifteen. And he would like to see the Ruth and Ronnie thing cleared up, one way or the other. Let the other boys keep busy with the legwork on that—on Wales, on Ritter—and see what turned up; he'd check this little idea himself. Just for fun.

He went home.

Overnight, he wondered what new little joke would turn up next morning. He was curious enough to call in at eight thirty, and got Rodriguez; but so far nothing had showed up. "Well, come to think he's had a busy three nights, hasn't he? Getting the pig into the Endlers' back yard on Friday night, and manhandling all those bottles on Saturday night, and setting the booby trap on Sunday night. I expect he needed some sleep. Maybe we'll get another one tomorrow. Or maybe Rasmussen getting hurt scared him. You and D'Arcy try to chase down these pals of Wales's, hm?"

"Just going out on it," said Rodriguez.

Maddox looked in the phone book and found a lot of listings under Packard-Bell Service Division, which sounded like what he was after. There were branches all over the county; he assumed the Hollywood one would be the relevant branch, and called there. He was passed around, finally got the service manager, and asked if there was any way of checking whether the same serviceman had visited a certain three homes at any time, and how often? The manager was very curious as to why the police should be interested.

"We try to keep a high quality of men, you know, Sergeant. Personally as well as—ah—technically. I can't believe that any of our men would be—ah—involved in anything the *police* might be—"

"I expect it'll be easier if I come round," said Maddox. "It's nothing like that, just a little thing I'm checking out."

"Oh," said the manager. "Oh, I see." He sounded puzzled. "Well, it will mean looking through a lot of back records, Sergeant, but I'll see what I can do."

"Fine. I'll be there in twenty minutes." Maddox put on a tie and his jacket, checked his pockets, and walked round the Clinton house to the Frazer-Nash at the curb.

The Hollywood branch was out on Melrose. Obviously it would service TV's in the area where the practical joker was operating. The manager, one Earl Meyers, turned out to be less pedantic than he'd sounded on the phone; Maddox rather took to him, and told him the whole story.

"Oh my God, that pig!" said Meyers, chuckling. "I saw *that* in last night's *Herald*." The pig had, true to D'Arcy's prophecy, got into the papers. "And these others— But, good Lord, Sergeant, you're not thinking any of *our* men could have—"

Maddox explained why it was just a possibility. "It looks just a little significant, doesn't it, that all three victims own Packard-Bell TV's and two of them carry insurance with you?"

Meyers bristled a little. "Not at all strange, Sergeant. Packard-Bell manufactures far and away the best machine on the market today, and our customers are increasing every day. Then too, many people prefer to buy a machine manufactured locally, if any trouble *does* arise— And then our insurance plan, of course—"

"Yes, I see. By the way, would the same men be apt to go out on—you know—calls to places where they had insurance, and also places they hadn't?"

"Oh yes. The calls for service just go on the schedule sheet and the next man free would— Well, I'm bound to say I can't agree that it's even *likely* one of our boys— What a thing! For

— 92

one thing, Sergeant," and Meyers grinned, "they work pretty hard—we don't have many slack days, I do assure you!—and I'd think they'd all need their sleep instead of gallivanting all over with pigs and— But if you'll give me the names of the people I'll check and see."

It took quite a little time, but all the calls were down in the records and eventually he gave Maddox two names. Don Forbes and Wayne Ericson. Both had visited all three houses, the Endlers', Fosters', and Rasmussens', on somewhat widely separated occasions. Other men had been at one or the other, and a couple at two of the places, but these were the only men who'd been at all three: and neither of them had visited any of the houses more than once, and the latest date either of them had been at any of those places wasn't recent: Forbes to the Rasmussens' four months back, and Ericson to the Fosters' two months back.

It was, however, something. Maddox would like to talk to both of them. He couldn't, immediately; both were out on calls.

Five minutes after Maddox had called, Rodriguez and D'Arcy were about to leave the office when the phone rang and Carter on the desk said this call sounded interesting. "Yes?" said Rodriguez.

"I'll put it through."

It was a man named Arnett. "Bill Arnett," said the cautious voice on the phone. "I got a place up here Pacoima Canyon, where I'm callin' from, just a little place, fifteen acres, unnerstand. I see in the papers last night about a hog."

"The pig?" said Rodriguez. "Oh yes, Mr. Arnett?"

"The hog. Yeah. That somebody painted and put polka

93 —

dots on, what a hell of a way treat a poor dumb animal. Even a hog. Well, I think it could be my hog, see. At least, it was."

"Oh. You had one stolen, or—"

"Well, I got—I had—six hogs. White Poland Chinas. Boar and five sows. They're inna yard, big yard all fenced acourse, 'bout seventy, eighty yards from the house. Little shack I got up here. O.K., that's last Thursday night. Friday morning I got five hogs. Boar and four sows. I do some cussing, and then damn if I don't happen to go round to the front door o' the house—I generally use the back door alla time, unnerstand—I went round there to the road to get in my car and go report I got a hog stolen to the cops, if you get me—"

"Yes?" said Rodriguez.

"And I notice somethin' white on the door so I go look. And damn if there's not an envelope fastened on the door with Scotch tape, and in it there's two fifty-dollar bills. You coulda knocked me down with a— Well, it was damn funny. Look, a guy wants to buy one o' my hogs, why don't he come say so face to face? Dicker with me? I'd prob'ly sold him the hog for a bit less 'n a hunderd. She was my own breedin'. But hell, so I figure, so what? It was a fair price. Only when I see in the papers about that one painted up, down Hollywood, I figure could be—"

"Yes, it probably was," said Rodriguez. "Yes, very funny indeed. Yes, thanks very much for calling in, Mr. Arnett." He put the phone down and told D'Arcy about that. "You know something, D'Arcy. This practical joker—money's no object with him. Now we hear this, and stop to think. A hundred bucks for the pig. He needn't have left that. And that gross of bottles, however he acquired them—what would that come to?"

D'Arcy thought. "They retail for eighty-nine cents each. That's—hell, where's some paper?" he scribbled. "A hundred and twenty-eight dollars and sixteen cents, for God's sake. And the book sold for six ninety-five."

"A piece of change to lay out. And all those children's toys looked new. And from what Dabney got—or didn't—he's a very canny one, wore gloves—nothing but smudges anywhere. He is going to one hell of a lot of trouble over his little jokes, isn't he? Well—" Rodriguez shrugged. "Not our business right now. Let's be on our way."

"I'm with you up to two," said D'Arcy. "Then I'm detailed to go play amateur theatricals with Carstairs, at that hotel."

"There are times," said Rodriguez, "when Ellis can be too damn stubborn. Look at the man hours he's spending just on that one thing! Well, come on, let's go try to prove Wales is lying."

"Huh?" said Wayne Ericson.

Maddox looked at him in exasperation. . . . It had certainly been an idea, and when the Packard-Bell link had showed up it had looked all the more suggestive. But he'd seen Don Forbes, when Forbes checked back at the office at noon to pick up any recent calls, and while you never knew, Forbes didn't look in the least like a man who'd be given to practical jokes. Even the unsubtle ones, and the boy they were after here had a fairly subtle sense of humor, didn't he?

Forbes was a big roughhewn fellow with hamlike hands and gentle brown eyes, and he'd seemed entirely bewildered at Maddox's questions, and sounded entirely honest. He had to think back to recall any of those calls—he didn't remember the names— "Look, we just get the addresses, and are they insured or not, that's all. We don't know the *people*, unless it's an old set needs fixing up pretty often. . . . Hear people talking? What do you mean, mister? I'm not deaf, sure I hear. Oh, like family arguments and so on? Well, sometimes and sometimes not, depends on the people, you know." He laughed. "I tell you one call I got, last month it was, like to have knocked me on my ass. You run into that sometimes too. This dame, she let me in, she's got nothing on but a kind of kimono held round her—real nice figure too—and she right away offers me a drink and hangs over me all the time I'm trying to work on the set—just dying I should make a pass, you know. Brother. Once in a while you run into that, but— What? What the hell you mean, like hearing about a guy drinks too much? I can't say I recall anything like that—you *do* once in a while run across a drunk, of course. Where was I *when?* What the hell you trying to do, connect me up with police business some kind? Friday night I was home asleep in bed with my wife, which is where I was Saturday night and Sunday night and come to that last night, and I'd just like to know why—"

And now Maddox was meeting Wayne Ericson, who looked if anything less likely to be the practical joker. He was a young man, and his extreme blondness and the bright blue of his eyes, his girlish mouth and slight build made him look younger than he probably was.

"Endler?" he said. "What was the other name you— No sir, I don't remember. If the record sheet says I was there, I was, but you don't remember the people, you know—you're busy on the set. . . . *Hear* anything? Oh, you mean like arguments or— Well, I don't recall anything like that. . . ."

Ericson was unmarried, and lived with his widowed mother.

He'd been out on a date on Saturday night; at home, so he said, Friday and Sunday nights. He seemed like a nice young fellow, but Maddox entertained serious doubts that there was much subtlety in him—or much humor.

He thanked them all and took himself away to a belated lunch. Waiting for it, he called the office and heard about Bill Arnett's peculiarly purchased sow. That gave him more to think about. Like Rodriguez, he realized belatedly that the practical joker was spending a tidy sum of money just for the fun of producing his jokes, which did not sound like a hard-working TV serviceman—even earning good union wages, probably a good deal more than Maddox's seven hundred odd per as an L.A.P.D. sergeant (and that the highest paid force anywhere, at that), neither Ericson nor Forbes would—

It was a very funny, offbeat thing, the practical joker. And Maddox didn't grudge him a full night's sleep, but he wondered curiously what the next one would be. A boy like this, there probably would be a next one.

Unless, of course, the unintentional injury to Rasmussen had scared him off.

The Packard-Bell thing. Coincidences. They did show up.

D'Arcy and Rodriguez were downtown, following a tangled trail. Wales, they'd discovered, had been somewhat less than frank about where he'd been on Friday night; it was in the cards he didn't really remember all of it.

They had a place to start: the girl, Ann, said he had left the house before she served dinner at six. They'd trailed him from there—backtracked him from Tony's Bar on Third where he had come in about eight o'clock. Fortunately he was pretty well known in that neck of the woods, and by stopping in every bar they'd been able to trace his movements fairly well.

About seven o'clock he'd visited a pawnshop on Second Avenue and hocked a woman's wristwatch for two fifty. Ann's, they surmised. They were also looking, of course, for Jimmy Russell and Al Dugan and Bob Cheevers, the pals Wales said he'd been with; he'd been alone at the pawnshop, but they found Cheevers—pointed out by the bartender—at a tavern on Main, and questioned him.

Cheevers one you might expect Wales to run with: another broken-down old bum. He shied away from cops, but they had him cornered and he answered them.

Yeah, sure he'd seen Tom Wales Friday night. Well, like in at Tony's. When? He guessed about nine o'clock. He hadn't stayed there, sure, Russell was there, same booth as Tom, and Dugan too. Sure he knew 'em all, but he'd just spoke a word or two, had a beer or maybe two, and he'd gone on. Home. He didn't know nothing about where else Tom went that night.

The bartender at Tony's knew Wales. "Damn old lush," he said, scowling. "One thing I can't stand's an old lush like that. No self-respect, you get me? We get a bunch of fellows here, regulars, nice fellows, they drop in awhile after work, in the evening, watch the TV, and talk, have a few beers—all quiet and nice. We got no fancy millionaires around here, plain honest working men, but quiet. You know? Nothing rough. I don't like these Skid Row types coming in. I tell the other barkeeps, Keep 'em waiting, discourage 'em like, you know? Like that. But I remember Wales and his two pals— same types. Sure. They had like maybe four beers apiece and they left about nine thirty. Around there. I tell you the truth, I was glad to see them go. I don't like—"

D'Arcy and Rodriguez wandered on, and presently found the next bar the three comrades had hit: the Four Aces on Los Angeles Street. There was a hiatus: that had been about ten thirty. The bartender there said they'd all been middling high.

"I don't like this," said D'Arcy. "The X on Ruth and Ronnie couldn't know how early they'd be getting home. I'd have said he'd be up there, lying in wait, by at least ten thirty or eleven, just in case. And we haven't got a smell on the gun."

"I know. It looked very hot, but I'm beginning to think Wales is just what he looks like—the lecherous old lush, period."

It was getting on for half past one then, and D'Arcy wished him luck, reclaimed his car from the parking lot at Central H.Q. (it was sometimes convenient to be a cop, avoiding parking charges), and started back for Hollywood to play amateur theatricals with Policewoman Carstairs. Rodriguez, bored to death with the routine legwork, went on hunting.

At three o'clock he found Jimmy Russell. Russell was a small cut above Wales and Cheevers: he had a job, laborer for the Southern Pacific. Washing the Pullman cars and so on. This was his day off, and he was sitting in a bar on Temple Street drinking beer. Again, the bartender knew him and pointed him out.

Russell was feeling amiable, and he wasn't nervous about cops; he was a friendly fellow, and the beer was making him feel friendlier.

"Rodriguez, hey?" he said. "I gotta say, you Latin guys got names that sound nice. Pretty. I studied Spanish at school—it's a right pretty-soundin' language. You're a right handsome fellow too, ain't you? Mustache and all. Funny how girls go for mustaches. I lost my best girl once to one o' you guys, fellow named Ricardo, but I don't bear no grudge."

Rodriguez asked him questions and Russell answered readily. Sure, he'd been with Tom Wales Friday night. And Al Dugan, too. Well, they'd gone here and there, none of them had much money, they'd just sort of wandered around. Well, it'd have been around midnight, he guessed, they went to this Black Cat Tavern, down on Temple, and that'd been their last stop. Place shut at one A.M.; they'd split, and gone home. At least, he'd gone home; he lived just over on Second, a nice rooming house there, nice landlady, he'd lived there ten years— "Not bein' married, see—that is, I got divorced a while back— I dunno what Al and Tom did, but Tom had his car and said he'd drive Al home, only he was pretty high and Al said better he should drive and Tom stay over with him, sober up, you know. Al lives somewhere out around First and Mission. You ain't thinkin' either of 'em *done* something? Neither of them do anything bad, Officer. Honest. Look, look, hey, I just remember, was a cop came in while we was there. See? In the bar. Cop in uniform. Just to look around, see there wasn't no trouble. He could say—"

Rodriguez went back to the big rectangular Police Facilities Building that was Central H.Q., and asked questions in the indicated place. They told him that the uniformed Traffic man on that beat Friday night would have been Patrolman Barnabas Tright, at present on night tour. They gave him Tright's address on Virgil Avenue.

Rodriguez went to see Tright, who had just got out of bed. Tright proved to be an alert young man, two years on the force, ambitious and very pleased to be able to help out a ranking detective.

"Sure, I remember that," he said. "We always run two-man cars down there, you know, but we were short last Friday on account Ed had this attack of appendicitis—Ed Murphy, my usual sidekick. He's in the hospital right now. So I was riding the tour alone, until the office shuffled things round and found me another partner next night. There are a couple of bars you automatically check once in a while—trouble spots, you know. Yeah, I remember going into the Black Cat."

"You remember seeing three middle-aged men together, all fairly well oiled?"

Tright thought. "One of them with a big stomach on him? He was just coming back from the men's room when I came in. He was loaded. If that was the three you mean, sir—I stopped that one, because I thought he was a prospect for the drunk tank, but one of his pals came up—he wasn't so high— and told me 'he and Jimmy' 'd take care of Tom, so I didn't take him in."

"Oh, really," sighed Rodriguez. "Just like that."

Tright eyed him. "Not what you wanted to hear?"

"Yes and no. Let's go down to the County Jail and have you look at somebody."

Tright identified Wales positively as the drunk he'd seen, and hadn't taken in. His report for Friday night clocked him as checking the Black Cat at five minutes to one A.M., just before it closed.

So Tom Wales hadn't been lurking behind the hedge on Franklin Avenue, waiting to shoot Ruth and Ronnie dead at approximately one fifteen A.M.

Rodriguez called Maddox at home at five o'clock to break

the bad news. "Hell and damnation!" said Maddox.

"I know. We'll go on looking at Ritter, but I'm wondering now if Ruth was the target. We haven't turned up any serious love angle on either of them, but it could be. And there's that Wedeck, on Ronnie—people do some damn funny things. For some damn funny reasons."

"Are you telling me?" said Maddox. "So tomorrow we take a closer look at Ritter. Not that anything showed up on him, what we got before. And maybe even—yes, it's *possible*—a look at this amorous landlord Sandra Bergstrom told us about. And all Ronnie's associates. His apartment's still sealed? I think I'll have another look there—forlorn hope. Damn. I'd like to get this bird. . . ."

He shaved and showered and went out to Sally Scott's party. Quite a girl, Sally. She distracted him a little bit from the cases, but not all the way.

Nine

So THEY WERE RIGHT BACK WHERE THEY'D STARTED ON RONNIE and Ruth, no real suspects (except Ritter, of course, and nothing tied him with the gun). They didn't know if X had meant to kill them both, or if only one, which. They hadn't a smell of any motive.

Who the hell had wanted to hurt or kill those two nice, respectable, responsible young people?

Maddox, for once, woke before the alarm sounded on Wednesday morning, and lay thinking about Ruth and Ronnie. It was a hell of a thing. He thought of a couple of new places to look for leads, and then he had a sudden idea that made him swear and get out of bed in a hurry.

He showed up at Wilcox Street at seven thirty and was regarded in surprise by Detectives Rowan and Feinman, offered facetious remarks. "I'm just a glutton for work," said Maddox, "that's all. Can hardly bring myself to leave the place, you know. Get your feet off my desk, Joe. Had a little idea. I'm occasionally a bit slow in the uptake."

"Occasionally, he says. And what's with Ellis, anyway? He's asked us both to do some overtime this afternoon, said he'd explain if we hung around till he came on."

"Yes, even using uniformed men he'll run out of new faces after a while. Though I suppose a couple of the johns could be expected to come back for more. He'll tell you." Maddox had been hunting his copies of the autopsy reports on Ruth and Ronnie. Finding them, he settled down to read the exact details of the injuries; his belated idea had been that their locations might possibly give him some clue as to which was the intended victim, or if both had been intended.

Ruth had been shot in the upper right shoulder, lower right chest, the right side of the neck, the right upper arm, and the upper right chest, that slug being deflected by bone and lodging near the heart. Ronnie had taken slugs in the upper left chest, left front shoulder, left cheekbone—that was the one that killed him, going on into the brain—and the left arm.

Well. Maddox was puzzled for a moment. How come all the shots in Ruth's right side and all on Ronnie's left? X had been aiming from over the hedge on the right side of the car. Maddox sat back and shut his eyes and visualized the scene. Yes, you could build it up. So D'Arcy was quite right, they'd been necking in the front seat. Ronnie had had his arms around the girl, turned toward her—more than she was toward him—when the bullets had hit. And that did say a little something, too. Didn't it say even stronger that Ruth was the intended target if only one had been? X would know she'd be in the passenger's seat, on the right side, and had therefore lain in wait to the right of the car.

On the other hand, there wasn't anything like that hedge, to provide cover, on the left of the drive—just the triple-terraced lawn down to the street; if X had waited, say, up by the house, he'd probably have been caught in the headlights as the car turned in the drive. He'd waited in the only place he could wait.

And if he'd primarily wanted Ronnie, all he'd have had to do would have been to lie in wait for him down on Ardmore Avenue. All right. Maddox still thought Ruth had been the target.

D'Arcy and Rodriguez came in together, and Rowan yawned and said, "Long night. Not a thing turned up for us." He got up and stretched.

"Ellis wants to see you," said D'Arcy.

"I know."

"What are you brooding over?" asked Rodriguez. Maddox opened his mouth to tell him, and the outside phone rang on his desk; he picked it up and said, "Maddox."

"Sir, I think you ought to come and—" it was a second before he identified the rather muffled voice as Stoner's—"and see this." Stoner gave a kind of strangled snort suddenly. "Excuse me—I mean, it's another of these—" again he stopped, and coughed, and said, suppressing what sounded like a giggle —if a big tough uniformed cop ever giggled—"by God, it looks so damn silly just sitting there—but the woman's having hysterics, her husband called their doctor, and anyway I thought you'd want to—"

"What is it this time?" asked Maddox curiously.

"Well, I guess you'd better come and see," said Stoner. "It's Citrus Avenue, just above Santa Monica." He added the address. And then he began to laugh helplessly and hung up.

"New joke," said Maddox. "Come on." He admitted to himself he was curious. What little human foible was being played on now?

Citrus Avenue—back in the neighborhood, right around the corner from Higman where the pink pig had wreaked such havoc.

When they got there, there was the squad car, a big black Buick with an M.D. sign on it, and a number of curious neighbors milling around. Stoner was standing at the gate—there was a chain-link fence around the house—keeping them out.

"Heard this screaming, I thought for sure the Russians had landed."

"Down at the end of the *block* I heard it, all I could think, My God, an accident, but there wasn't any crash. What's wrong with Mrs. Burdick, anyway? She—"

"Mr. Burdick said she was scared, I heard him tell the—"

They pushed through the little crowd and Stoner let them in the gate. "My God," he said. "Wait till you see." The house was an old one, very well kept up: one of the early California bungalows with a good-sized side porch and side door—that generally gave entrance to the dining room—as well as a front porch. There was a little cement walk, branching off from the main front walk, leading around to the side porch, and Stoner led them that way.

"The woman—Mrs. Burdick—didn't come into the dining room till about half an hour ago, see, Sergeant. It's next to the side porch. And when she did—her husband was in the bathroom shaving and he said he damn near cut his throat when she started to scream—well, she saw *that* through the glass door, and—" He stopped; they all stopped.

That was propped sitting, looking oddly relaxed and comfortable, in an old wicker rocking chair on the porch. It was a nice specimen—so far as they could tell—of a fully articulated skeleton, and it was sitting there, leaning back in the chair against a shabby green cushion, one leg draped over the other; it had an old plaid shawl around its shoulders, and on the bony fleshless skull there sat, rather rakishly, a battered old felt hat. And it was holding a folded newspaper in both hands.

They all began to laugh. The damn thing did look so silly just sitting there, and yet completely natural and somehow lifelike too. Maddox went up closer. The joker had gone to infinite trouble to get the effect he wanted: the newspaper had been affixed to the hands with Scotch tape, and more tape held the shawl in place; thin white twine had been used to tie the legs in their insouciant position, and under the shawl the naked ribs were tied to the back of the chair.

"Oh my God!" said Rodriguez, still laughing. "But what's the point? I don't—" And a tall thin man stepped out to the porch from the side door, and looked from them to Stoner.

"Er—Sergeant Maddox, sir. This is Mr. Burdick."

"Well, what about all this, Mr. Burdick? I understand your wife—" Resolutely Maddox looked away from the jaunty skeleton.

"What about it indeed," said Burdick. He was a man about forty, not bad-looking, dark. "I'd like to know who—what a trick to—" And then he looked at the skeleton and began to laugh. "Heartless," he gasped, "poor Irene so damn upset—but when I first—oh my God!—saw it, all I could think was, Goddamn, just what the old boy'd do if he could! Oh, would he have got a kick out of this! Excuse me—" He straightened, wiping his eyes. "Doctor's giving her a sedative. Of course, you don't know, but— Well, it was somebody who knew him, that I'll say. I'll be damned if whoever did it hasn't got that fool thing sitting there exactly the way he used to sit—same kind of shawl and hat and all. Exactly. When I first saw it—

my God, I nearly slashed my throat when Irene started to sound off, talk about sirens, I—"

"Who, Mr. Burdick? This—"

Burdick chuckled. "The old man—my uncle, Uncle Bart Beckwith. He was quite a character, Uncle Bart. Been everywhere, done everything—but all he had was the pension. Well, hell, I liked the old chap and besides I was his only relative, he'd never married. And I'll say that Irene tried to control herself, because she's not a mean woman, but she resented him being here like hell. Upset her nice orderly house. Said he embarrassed her, all her friends thought he was so funny and eccentric, and of course he was around all the while, he was pretty lame, and he used to sit out here, in this very chair, practically all day—with a plaid shawl just like that round his shoulders—except in summer, naturally—and he was a friendly old cuss, he'd call out to anybody passing, come up and talk to him—and Irene said it looked queer. He knew the mailman by his first name, and all the kids on the block, like that. And he had a couple of old cronies used to come and see him, one of them chewed tobacco too, and Irene just couldn't abide— She'd blow off steam to me at night, he made people think we were queer, and talking to everybody, and spitting tobacco juice in her flower bed by the porch. Well, you know women! She was so damn relieved when he died last September. Well, I know the old boy was odd, maybe, but I liked him, he was nearly ninety and still pretty bright. He—" Burdick looked at the skeleton, chuckling. "I guess she'd been feeling a little bit guilty about how she'd talked about him, treated him, and then when she saw *that*—oh my God, when I saw it, all I could think was, *Just* what the old boy'd do, annoy Irene one last time! Oh my God—just exactly how he used to sit, with those old Congress gaiters showing and his long-john under-wear—"

They all looked at the skeleton and started to laugh all over again. The skeleton seemed to stare back, grinning.

A short fat little man came around the side walk; he was carrying a medical bag. "Oh, there you are, Mr. Burdick. Well, your wife'll be quite all right—just momentary shock. And in a way, no wonder." He stared at the skeleton and shook his head. "Very heartless sort of joke to play. You're—er—police? I suppose you'll be looking into it. Juveniles, possibly."

"Ah—Doctor," said Maddox, "would it be very easy for a private person to acquire a prepared skeleton like that?"

"Possibly." The doctor walked up and peered at the skele-ton. "It's an ordinary articulated skeleton such as you'd see in any medical school—places like that. There'd be any number of them around—old-fashioned doctors sometimes kept one in their offices. Or it may have been stolen from somewhere." He shrugged and started for his car.

Burdick said, "I suppose you'll take it away?" He looked at it. "Damn if it doesn't make me feel sort of homesick for the old boy. Sure to God, whoever put it there knew him. You can see why it upset Irene."

They didn't particularly want the skeleton, but of course it would have to be gone over for prints.

" 'Behold, a pale horse,' " said Maddox, back at the office. "Joker this time gently pointing out to Irene that we do all come to it. This is being a damn nuisance. Just jokes, doing no harm, but we've got to do a little looking—and now Ruth and Ronnie coming to pieces on us." He looked at his watch; both the funerals were being held today and he wanted to go to both or at least see somebody went; sometimes you picked up a lead at a funeral. An idea, the way somebody was behaving or talking.

Ruth's at the Church of the Recessional at Forest Lawn at eleven. Ronnie's at Temple Sinai in Hollywood at three.

They would now go to see all Ruth's friends again, and they hadn't looked up many of Ronnie's; lean on Ritter a little, hope to get something definite there one way or the other; look at all Ruth's cases again. And Maddox thought suddenly, depressingly—considering the prevalence of Neanderthal in a metropolis this size—and also the number of hopped-up juveniles—it could have been, could merely have been, somebody full of dope with a gun, a nut with a gun, a juvenile with a gun—just there by chance, to shoot off the gun at somebody for fun. You got that sort of wanton thing. Sometimes.

He asked Rodriguez to cover Ruth's funeral. He told them about his brainstorm on the positions of the slugs, and they both agreed with his conclusions. It didn't really say much. He thought he'd try to find Ritter and have a little session with him, and he was just about to leave the office when a young Negro came in hesitantly and asked, "Is this—are you the detectives? The desk sergeant said—"

"We are. What can we do for you? I'm Sergeant Maddox. Detectives D'Arcy—Rodriguez."

"Well, it's about Ronnie. Ronnie Morgenstern. I should say, my name's Williams, Edward Williams." He came in farther, and on invitation sat down beside Maddox's desk. "I'm going to L.A.C.C. too, I was in some of his classes and I knew him. Just casually, you know—oh, we'd eat lunch together in the cafeteria, coffee breaks, like that." Williams was a tall, medium-brown young man with the Semitic features of North

African ancestry; quite good-looking. He was dressed neatly in dark-blue slacks, open-necked white shirt. "I didn't *believe* it when I heard— Ronnie Morgenstern getting murdered! Didn't seem like anything could happen. I never heard about it till this morning, because my dad got hurt in an accident up near Fresno, Friday it was—he drives a truck for Interstate Movers—and I had to take my mother right up there, we only got home last night. He's not bad, be out of the hospital another couple of days, now. Well, when I got to the college this morning and heard about Ronnie—that's one hell of a thing, he was a nice guy, you know, nicest guy you'd want to meet—and killing his girl too! What kind of nut would— Well, anyway, I don't know if it'll mean anything to you, but I thought I'd better come in and tell you. Not that I want to get anybody in trouble, least of all me," and he grinned briefly, "and if he's got nothing to do with it and finds I sicked the cops on him, I'd likely meet trouble. But Ronnie was a nice guy. What it is, he'd had a little trouble with this fellow, I happened to know."

"Oh? What fellow?"

"His name's Offenbach. I don't think he's the owner of the place, just a clerk—there's another man there sometimes, an older man, I heard him call this other one Offenbach. It's a place out on Western, secondhand books and magazines, and I've been there with Ronnie—sometimes he drove me home if we left at the same time. And this place stocks a lot of textbooks and stuff like that, only place around here does, secondhand, reason a lot of the college people go there. I don't suppose Ronnie would have, if there'd been another place as well stocked, because this Offenbach, well, he was always coming out with snide remarks, you know, about kikes and so forth—

and he doesn't like *us* so damn much either," said Williams, looking amused.

"Only the superior white et cetera entitled to an education?" said Rodriguez.

"I guess. Well, the trouble that came up, it was stupid, but I just got to thinking, one like this Offenbach maybe wouldn't need much reason to— I don't know. You see, there was this old man, a pensioner, lived near where Ronnie did, and it shows you the kind of fellow Ronnie was—he liked the old man, felt sorry for him, he hasn't any family, lives alone. Busy as he was and all, Ronnie used to go visit the old man a couple of evenings a week, play checkers, bring him paperbacks and magazines." Williams paused. "I tell you, Ronnie had what they call empathy, you know? Put himself in the other person's place, understand feelings. He felt sorry for the old man. Well, a couple of paperbacks he bought at this place, for the old man, it turned out half the pages were missing, and he called this clerk on it, said the books ought to be checked before they're put out for sale—which seems reasonable—and they had a hell of an argument. I was there—this was just last Thursday."

"Oh really?" said Maddox, sitting up.

"That's right. It sounds like nothing at all, but when I heard about Ronnie— Well," said Williams, "there was that thing a couple of months back, two fellows in a bar arguing over who'd pay the check, and one of 'em shot the other dead. You see the crazy things like that."

"People being people," said D'Arcy thoughtfully.

"That's right," said Williams. "And this Offenbach—you know, I wouldn't doubt that he's maybe one of those American Nazis—he really blew his top at Ronnie for complaining

— 112

about that. Called him every name in the book—I mean, and he *knew* them. And the look in his eye— Well, I tell you no lie, once I was expecting him to jump the counter and go for Ronnie with both hands. I was getting ready to you might say pitch in to the rescue, when I thinks, Uh-uh, couple of members of the minority groups, like they say, we get some of these nuts starting a riot." Williams grinned. "And anyway—"

"How did Ronnie react?"

"Well, Ronnie had his head screwed on," said Williams soberly. "It's kind of awkward sometimes to have a logical mind. I'm a law student too, by the way. You have that kind of mind, you just naturally expect other people to see logic too, and, man, they just don't always."

"How well I know what you mean," murmured Rodriguez. Maddox laughed.

"Ronnie started out talking logic to the fellow, but when Offenbach sort of blew up in his face, you could put it, he saw he wasn't about to get anywhere with him and he just tried to calm him down. If you get me. It didn't do any good. Offenbach just got madder. He was really worked up—nearly foaming at the mouth. Mostly about dirty Christ-killing kikes having the nerve to complain to him. Like that. Finally Ron just said to me, 'Come on, Ed,' and walked out. Now I know it sounds like nothing. But I got to thinking, and you take these real fanatics like this Offenbach—"

"And sometimes it takes really nothing to set them off, yes," said Maddox. "That's all very interesting, Mr. Williams —thanks very much for coming in to tell us about it."

"I just thought you'd better hear. In case," said Williams. . . .

And instead of starting out to find Ritter, Maddox continued to sit at his desk, and he said thoughtfully, "So, considering Mr. Offenbach—who I'd like to see—another small idea occurs to me. We've checked Frank Gates, but her former boy friends didn't look very likely—up to now—and we haven't really looked for them. But she was a pretty girl. If serious. I'm wondering now—even in these enlightened days, we do still find them—if somebody who'd dated Ruth, maybe been crazy about Ruth and been given the brush-off—wasn't maybe feeling very damn annoyed and frustrated and what-have-you, not just because Ruth had got engaged but because she'd got engaged to a dirty Christ-killing kike."

"Well, a thought," said Rodriguez. "Could be. What do we do about it?"

"Talk to all her girl friends. Women I know a little something about. Even serious, dedicated girls like Ruth, they talk about the opposite sex to girl friends. The ones they're dating, have dated. So some one of those may come out with something. . . . I think I'll go see this Offenbach. D'Arcy, suppose you—"

"Por Dios, that funeral," said Rodriguez. "It's ten thirty. I'm off," and he snatched up his hat and ran out.

Maddox got up and the inside phone rang on his desk. He picked it up resignedly. "Mad—"

"Bank job at the Security-First, Highland and Hollywood," said Carter tersely. "Squad car just called in. Finch and Gomez. They were cruising and heard the shots—hit it fast, and Gomez copped one, ambulance on the way, and a teller—"

"For God's sake!" said Maddox. "All right, we're on it. D'Arcy—"

So they were busy on that for quite some time. When they

got to the bank, the ambulance had just arrived; Gomez wasn't bad, had a slug in one shoulder. He said he thought he'd hit one of them. The teller wasn't so good: young woman, two bullets in her chest.

And people—my God, people, thought Maddox. Nineteen people in the bank at the time, aside from nearly thirty employees on the ground floor: they had to get statements from all of them, and what had those nearly fifty people seen? As per usual, nearly fifty different descriptions they got.

Added up, it led to some deductions, a few definite things. Three bank robbers. One tall, fat, middle-aged: khaki pants, khaki shirt. One young, slim, short, with curly hair. One very vaguely described man who'd stayed by the door; the only thing most witnesses agreed on there was that he'd had a long gun—a sawed-off shotgun maybe, said one man—anyway not a handgun, maybe a rifle, maybe a shotgun—

"Maybe a machine gun," grunted D'Arcy.

The big fat man had had a gun too. A revolver. Or an automatic. Most of the witnesses didn't know the difference. Apparently he'd put the gun on the chief teller, and she'd kept her head, started to hand over the money. But a pretty little brown-haired girl named Agnes Bailey, a new employee, had come up to ask the chief teller something while that was going on, and seeing the gun had panicked, screamed, and run—so of course the chief teller was the one who got shot. And Finch and Gomez had heard the shots, cruising outside, and come in fast, and some more shots had been exchanged as the bank robbers ran out.

"I think I got one," Gomez said as they'd loaded him on the stretcher. "Little guy about five-six, curly blond hair—dark pants, blue shirt—"

And a man who'd been dropping a letter into a mailbox outside the bank said all three men had run out and dived into a tan car parked in a loading zone there. He said, a tan Mercury, 1959 or 1960, but of course he hadn't got the plate number.

They put out a call on the car, which would probably come to nothing with that rather vague description. They rushed the slugs up to Ballistics—the one out of Gomez, the two out of the chief teller. The one out of Gomez, Ballistics said, was from a Smith and Wesson Masterpiece .32. The two slugs out of the chief teller (a thirty-four-year-old woman with three children, incidentally) were from a Colt .357 Magnum. Nice to know. Sometime, maybe, helpful.

They took a lot of witnesses down to Central H.Q., to look at a lot of mug shots in Records. Who could say what would come of that, eyewitnesses being what they were? They took statements.

They did the routine that had to be done. As far as the Ruth and Ronnie thing went, they wasted most of the day. Just so many of them—to do the routine that had to be done.

And even so, Ellis snatching men off Traffic detail to don plain clothes and go play amateur theatricals with Police-woman Carstairs at the Golden Cock.

The thankless job—

Maddox missed Ronnie's funeral: sent Donaldson to cover it. At four thirty he drove out to Ardmore Avenue, and found the Goldfarbs and Mrs. Barker and a weeping elderly man holding a wake in Ronnie's apartment.

Ten

"I SUPPOSE I SHOULDN'T RIGHTLY HAVE BROKEN THAT SEAL YOU put on the door," said Mrs. Barker, wiping her eyes, "but here's Mr. and Mrs. Goldfarb wanting to clear up Ronnie's things and all, and it didn't seem right I should—"

"Well, I suppose it doesn't matter much," said Maddox. After all, they'd had a thorough look around here once; it wasn't likely they'd missed anything of significance.

Mrs. Goldfarb sat on the couch and sobbed. Goldfarb, very decorous in a black suit and tie, looked tired and withdrawn. He was making rather futile attempts to soothe the old man, who turned out to be Robert Rhys, the pensioner Ronnie had felt sorry for, played checkers with.

"Just like my own son, that boy—nobody'll ever know how I loved that boy, Mr. Goldfarb." Tears poured down Rhys's face. He was a small old man, only a little bent, and he'd kept a full head of fluffy white hair. They'd all just come from the funeral; he wore a dark suit too, but shabby, and his black tie had obviously just been bought for the occasion. "If you knew how he'd cheered my life the last few years—a good boy, take time to come and talk with me. Folks are kind, but they're busy, you know—like Mrs. Waterman, my landlady, kind as can be but most people don't take the time. But Ronnie—Ronnie—it's not right, Mr. Goldfarb—such a good boy!"

"Nothing about it makes any sense, Mr. Rhys," said Goldfarb heavily. He looked at Maddox. "I'm sorry, I didn't realize there was a seal on the door, sir, but—"

"It's all right," said Maddox.

"Just no *sense*," said Goldfarb. "Have you got anywhere on it yet?"

"I've got to go along with you—doesn't seem to be any rhyme nor reason to it. We've had some leads, I've got another one now, but they've all been dead ends."

"It must have been some nut, is all I can think," said Goldfarb. "Just a nut loose with a gun. In a place this size—could be you'll never find who."

"You know we'll keep on trying, Mr. Goldfarb. I'd very much like to get this one. What I—"

"Took the *time*, that was it," Rhys was going on. He brought out an enormous white handkerchief and blew his nose. "It isn't often you find a young person sympathetic and kind like that. I'm just an old man, well, I knocked around a little, railroading and such, when I was younger, I've got a few tales to tell, but it isn't often at all you find a young person like that to take time, listen to you, chat with you. A good boy. Nobody'll ever know how much I thought of Ronnie."

What Maddox wanted to know—and he was as pleased to find the Goldfarbs here, he wanted to ask them too—was whether Ronnie had said anything to Mrs. Barker about that argument with the bookstore clerk. He hadn't.

"Had you heard anything from him about that, Mr. Goldfarb?"

Goldfarb shook his head. "I hadn't talked to him since, I

think it was Wednesday—week ago today. He was coming out to have dinner with us Sunday. What'd you say happened?"

"Mr. Goldfarb, I don't like to ask you, but it'd mean an awful lot to me if I could have a little something of Ronnie's, just as a memento like," said Rhys. "Oh, I don't mean anything valuable, I wouldn't ask for anything. But maybe—maybe his pen? The one he always used. You'll never know how I'm going to miss that boy." He was still crying gently.

Goldfarb patted his arm. "Now, Mr. Rhys. I know that—he'd told us about you, he liked you—he went to see you because he liked you, not just he was sorry for you, you know. He said you were an interesting talker."

"He did? He said that?"

"And sure you can have a keepsake. His pen, you want it." Goldfarb found it on the desk, a well-worn Parker 51, and pressed it into Rhys's hand. "We know you thought a lot of him."

"Thank you, sir, thank you. I—I expect I'd better get home and not bother you more." He got up slowly, mopping at his eyes, clutching the pen. "Thank you. It just doesn't seem to make sense—good boy like that."

"I'll just see him on his way," said Mrs. Barker, starting after him. "He's in a state, no wonder, poor old fellow, and he's had one stroke already." She went after him.

Maddox sat down and told Goldfarb about the bookstore clerk. "I'm on my way to check him. Ronnie hadn't mentioned him?"

Goldfarb sighed, took off his glasses, and began to polish them with his handkerchief. "I wonder," he said, "if we will ever see the last of it, Sergeant—the hate and the intolerance and the damn silly lies people can be got to listen to. Sometimes you think it's dying out, you don't run into it much any more, and then again something like this—and you wonder. When the hell, Sergeant, are we going to all use common sense and admit we all come good, bad, and indifferent? Me, I happen to be an honest man. As honest as any of us come. But for God's sake, I'm not honest or dishonest, or for that matter a Republican or a Mason or any other damn thing I happen to be, because I'm a Jew—just because I'm me, Ben Goldfarb. Nor I don't suppose you're the smart cop you look like, or vote the way you do, or keep the kind of morals you do, because your ancestors were Scotch or English or whatever—"

"Welsh," said Maddox. "No. But at any given time, you know, there are a hell of a lot of illogical-minded people walking around loose."

"And that is the truth," said Goldfarb. He put his glasses back on. "And if it was for *that*—this—this Nazi just losing his temper— Here in this country, this year. I don't know, Sergeant." He studied one spatulate, workworn hand. "My grandfather came here, back in eighteen forty-seven, from Berlin. I always figured we'd all been pretty good citizens. But if you learn one thing, you get to be sixty-seven, it's that things just don't always make sense, the way they come out. . . ."

It had started life as a big garage, and been converted to a shop. Well-stocked you could say: shelves ran to the ceiling round all four sides except for a narrow partition at the rear where evidently a small office had been enclosed. The shelves were packed with books, paperback and hardcover. Most of the shelves had hand-lettered signs tacked on, indicating subject matter.

There was a desk bearing a cash register, at the rear of the store, and a clerk sitting at the desk. There were some half-dozen people in the place, browsing or searching the shelves, and all but one of them, Maddox noticed, were of college age, probably all students.

He went up to the desk. The clerk looked bad-tempered even before he spoke; he had a bitter, down-turned, thin mouth, narrow suspicious eyes under lowering eyebrows, and two deep indentations ran from mouth-corner to jaw. He was entirely bald, about fifty. He had on khaki pants and a once-white shirt.

He looked up at Maddox. "Help you find something?" he asked ungraciously.

Maddox showed him his badge and the narrow eyes turned wary. "So what are you after here?"

"Is your name Offenbach by any chance?"

"And so what the hell if it is?" asked the clerk belligerently.

"I understand you had quite an argument in here last Thursday with one of the customers," said Maddox. "He'd made some complaint and evidently you didn't feel he had a right to. Young man named Morgenstern—Ronald Morgenstern."

"Yeah? Well, still so what?" The eyes were wary and very cold.

"Well, you see, Mr. Morgenstern was shot the following night," said Maddox gently. "Shot and killed, Mr. Offenbach. Also his fiancée, who was with him. And I'd like to know where you were and what you were doing at the time, Mr. Offenbach."

"Me? You're trying to pin a murder—" Offenbach stepped back to the door in the partition wall. "Mr. Kramer. Could you come out a minute?"

Maddox looked at the newcomer with interest. He was a man about Offenbach's age, tall and slender, meticulously dressed, and on the surface his manner was easy and affable, but his oddly-light blue eyes never changed expression. . . . "Argument?" he said. "Oh yes, I recall you mentioned that, John. You really should control your temper better." He smiled at Maddox. "But really, sir, as to *killing* a man—you are really grasping at straws there. John? A little argument? This— I didn't get the name."

"Morgenstern. You didn't see it in the papers?"

"Yes, now you recall it to my mind I believe I did. I—"

"He had been a regular customer here," said Maddox; when Williams had told him the name of the store he'd recognized it, from Ronnie's checkbook. There had been at least one check written in payment of a purchase here, and the checks in Ronnie's checkbook were personal ones, of course, from the Bank of America, printed clearly in the upper left-hand corner with his name and the address on Ardmore Avenue. "He'd written checks to you, so you'd have known his name."

"We do have a good many customers," said Kramer, his light eyes unwavering.

"Does Mr. Offenbach make a habit of having slanging matches with the ones he doesn't like? A witness has described him as—um—nearly foaming at the mouth and calling Morgenstern every name in the book."

"That goddamned uppity black boy—"

"Oh really, John. That temper of yours— But I'm afraid you lower my previously good opinion of our police force, Sergeant, if you are really suspecting Mr. Offenbach of *murder* on such a vague story! But I'm sure he'll be able to satisfy you of his innocence. Er—when did the homicide take place?"

"At one fifteen A.M. on Saturday morning," said Maddox, watching him.

"Ah!" said Kramer. "How very fortunate. Then I can assure you personally that he could have had nothing to do with it. We have been working quite late here the last week. I have just purchased a large library, an estate sale, and it was not catalogued at all, so we have had quite a tedious job on our hands. One fifteen A.M., you said? Yes. At that time, Sergeant, Mr. Offenbach and I were both here, as was another clerk I employ part time, Joseph Kyser."

"I see," said Maddox. "That's very definite."

"I shall be glad to give you Mr. Kyser's address, you can—"

"Trying to pin a murder on me—"

"Thanks so much," said Maddox, and turned and walked out. None of the customers had paid any attention to that little scene.

He got into the Frazer-Nash and lit a thoughtful cigarette. Well, he thought, if you didn't ask questions you got no answers. He started the car and drove down to the Hall of Justice, looked at the board in the lobby, and found the office of the F.B.I.

A calm-eyed receptionist looked at his badge and asked him what he wanted. "Somebody," said Maddox, "to answer a couple of questions. About local subversive organizations."

"I think Mr. Morgan is free, Sergeant. Room two along the corridor, I'll buzz him to say you're on the way."

Mr. Morgan was the usual impeccably groomed, bland-eyed Fed. He offered Maddox a hand and said, "What can I do for the home-town boys, Sergeant? Sit down."

Maddox sat down and asked, "Does the name of John—probably Johann originally—Offenbach ring any bells in your head? Or Kramer— I don't know his first name? Or Joseph Kyser?"

"Nice and loud," said Morgan. "Three bells. What the hell's your interest?"

Maddox told him. "I'm not asking any questions about what you've got on them," he added hastily. "I know it's not allowed. But it looked very fishy to me, that pat alibi. And I know it's no motive at all for such a wholesale shooting party, but we do so often get the wanton killings. And Offenbach apparently flies off the handle pretty easy and feels pretty strongly about Jews."

"And a few other groups," said Morgan. He made a steeple of his hands and stared into space. Then he picked up a phone on his desk and said, "Ask Elliott to come in here, will you. . . . This might be helpful. Those three, we're fairly sure, are the instigators of a little hate group that's sprung up just the last few months—Citizens for Peace, I ask you—and we think they're responsible for a lot of nasty propaganda sheets getting circulated around—you know the sort of thing. But we haven't been able to tie any of them up to wherever the stuff's being printed. And we like to think we're pretty good, too, but they've shaken their tails time after time. Offenbach is, or was, a printer."

"Oh," said Maddox.

"We've got nothing on any of them but suspicion. Kramer we keep an eye on automatically—he's a former member of the American Nazis and was interned during the war as a security risk. God knows what he's been up to since. He's a very cautious bird, we haven't got any evidence on him. But now your business— Oh, Elliott. Sergeant Maddox, one of the local boys." He outlined the situation to Elliott, another tall bland Fed—was it the training made them all so alike?

"Offenbach," said Elliott. "You know, you might not be woolgathering at that, Sergeant. He's got a record for violence, and not just for losing his temper and going for somebody right then and there. Reason he got booted out of the union, he had a fight with another fellow over politics, and he not only beat him up at the time, he went out and set fire to his house the next night. They all got out all right, but it was a near thing. He did a one-to-three on arson for that. I can see Offenbach, what we know of him, just maybe thinking it'd be fun to gun down the damn kike who'd complained to him."

"And do you think, Dave—" said Morgan. "That is, Sergeant Maddox needn't—if he'll cooperate—mention that he's been offered a substantiated alibi? On a possible homicide charge—"

Maddox looked at them. "Well," he said temperately, "this force does have a reputation for what's called integrity, and I've always been a reasonably honest cop. Why—"

Elliott sighed and hoisted one hip to the corner of Morgan's desk. "We have to operate within the law just like you boys. And you don't need telling, some of the decisions getting handed down lately about prisoners' rights and suspects' rights and information received—"

"Oh, please," said Maddox. "You'll spoil my appetite for dinner. Information received—for Christ's sake, that one. I ask you, how unrealistic can you get?" He thought about that bitterly: conferences and new briefings of all law-enforcement officers going on all over the state. The damn ivory-tower legislators putting it on the books, any information gathered from police informers, the officer must reveal the name of said informer when the charge was made, stand ready to produce same. Unrealistic!—a lot of cases always broken by the stool pigeons, but by nature they were shy birds, and when they knew they'd be fingered in open court, every damn one of them shutting up for good and all. "Never mind, boys," he said wryly, "I don't think I'll get time for dinner anyway. We haven't caught up to those bank robbers yet."

"Yeah, we've got a few men out on that too. You see," said Elliott, "we haven't been able to get a search warrant for their living quarters—Kramer, Kyser, and Offenbach, I mean. We've got the store tapped, all illegal, but nothing's shown, and they all live in the same apartment building, out on Cahuenga, and we haven't been able to get in there at all, legal or otherwise. There's a very eagle-eyed manageress and when she's out she leaves her daughter on guard. Name of Von Kreuger."

"Do tell," said Maddox.

"If we could get a search warrant, all legal, even for only one of them—" said Morgan wistfully.

"Well," said Maddox, "I'm all for justice, if we have to go round the back roads to get it. Let me try for one, anyway." He looked at his watch; it was five forty-seven. He got up.

"Tell you what," said Morgan, "I'll invite you both to dinner while we wait for it. Because I've got a hunch—I've *just* got a hunch—"

Maddox got the warrant.

Morgan took them out to Mike Lyman's while they waited for it, and they celebrated with drinks beforehand.

At seven o'clock they drove, in Morgan's new Ford, up to Cahuenga Avenue and the newish small apartment house— eight units—where Kramer, Kyser, and Offenbach lived. The manageress was a hard-eyed blonde by request who looked at the warrant with sullen angry eyes, produced a passkey grudgingly, and instantly retreated into her own apartment, slamming the door.

"Gone to call Kramer," said Morgan. They went upstairs. A pity they hadn't any evidence to ask for warrants to search Kramer's and Kyser's places; be grateful for what they had. . . .

"O frabjous day!" said Morgan fifteen minutes later. "Look what I've found!" A stack of just-printed stuff from the closet in Offenbach's bedroom. The same tired old stuff. The Great Jewish Conspiracy. Racial Purity Demands Action Now. The Catholic Menace. Badly printed on poor-quality paper, but there was still—lamentably—a segment of the population it would reach.

"Oh, how very nice," said Elliott. "How very nice! Look, Bob, there's an address—" he whipped out a notebook—"Van Owen Street. Important speech by Dr. Henry Kramer—he started out as Hans, didn't he?—no admission, November twenty-first— Sounds like a private address. Now we can—"

But Maddox had just made a discovery of his own. It was a small apartment, the rooms cramped. One bedroom, if it had a walk-in closet, a short hall, bath, tiny kitchen, living room— in the hall was a linen cupboard, quite small, with double doors. Morgan busy in the bedroom closet, Maddox opened the linen cupboard for a routine look, and stared.

"Well, well, just look at this," he said.

Elliott continued to pore rapturously over their find; Morgan came to look and said, "Good God Almighty! Are they planning on starting a revolution?"

There were a lot of guns in the linen cupboard. In fact, nothing else but guns. Mostly handguns, but some others. There was a nine-millimeter Mauser rifle, three Savage big-game rifles, a Weatherby Mark V rifle, and a Marlin thirty-thirty. There was—they were sorting them out carefully—an S. and W. K-Masterpiece .22 target revolver, a Colt Match Target .22 automatic, a Ruger .357 magnum, a Ruger Single-

Six .22, a Walther Mark II .380 automatic, a Colt Python .357 magnum, an S. and W. 955 target .45, an S. and W. .44 magnum, a Ruger Black Hawk .357 magnum, a Colt Peacemaker revolver, .44 caliber, a Colt single-action army revolver, .45 caliber, an S. and W. nine-millimeter automatic, a Colt Super .38 automatic, and—"Are prayers sometimes answered?" said Maddox, pleased—and an S. and W. 1950 army model revolver, chambered for .45 ACP cartridges.

"Don't say that's the equalizer you're looking for on Morgenstern?"

"Oh, but it is," said Maddox. "Yes, indeed. So Ballistics told us. Of course quite a few of them were made, there'll be quite a few floating around, but still it's nice to find one in Mr. Offenbach's possession." He looked at it tenderly. "I needn't ask you not to touch it." He went looking, and in the kitchen wastebasket found an empty shoe box. He brought it back to the hall and, using his pen and pocketknife, maneuvered the revolver into the bottom half of the box. "I don't think I'll take any bets," he said, "that it's the same S. and W. 1950 army model that took off Ruth and Ronnie. No. I've been a cop long enough to know that it doesn't often come that easy. But maybe—"

Elliott was still chortling happily over the pamphlets. Some definite charge now—if they could make it stick. The damn judges—

"Well, it could be," said Morgan. "I'll keep my fingers crossed for you." And a key snicked in the lock of the front door. They turned.

Offenbach charged in already shouting, "What the goddamn hell a search warrant you guys can't— You just get the hell out of my place. Christ-damn dirty snoopers—you—"

"Hold it right there!" said Morgan, reaching for his gun, but before he touched it Offenbach was on him. He wasn't a boxer, he hadn't any technique but bull force; he sent Morgan flying over backward by sheer weight, and fell on top of him and began pommeling him wildly, screaming obscenities.

"What the hell—" Elliott had been in the bedroom, came at a run.

Maddox took one stride and reached to haul Offenbach up by the collar of his shirt. He heard the shirt rip under his hand. He heard, quite clearly, Benjamin Goldfarb saying, "I always figured we'd all been pretty good citizens." He thrust Offenbach around to a nice easy position, and judging the distance with an experienced eye he took him on the point of the jawbone with all the force in him.

Offenbach flew backward two feet and collided with Elliott. They both went down flat and all the breath came out of Elliott in a strangled *whoosh* as Offenbach landed on him.

Morgan went to untangle them. Elliott sat up and made crowing noises. "Sorry," said Maddox, licking his right knuckles, "I didn't see you coming."

Morgan, squatting over Elliott, turned and stared at him. "You can't be much more than a middleweight. For God's—"

"Around a hundred and forty," said Maddox.

"He'll have a good thirty pounds on you," said Morgan, sounding stunned. "You all right, Dave?"

"I expect so," said Maddox. He looked at Offenbach, flat on his back and dead out. "I don't like that man," he said mildly.

"Oh really," said Morgan. "You—uh—ever do any boxing, Sergeant?"

Maddox shook his head. "Just a little fighting. When the

occasion warrants it." He looked at his raw knuckles and then grinned at Morgan. "And I should be telling a guy named Morgan it's a Welsh name? We don't grow the biggest men, but pound for pound— And we tend to have kind of strong opinions."

He sent the gun down to Ballistics, and asked priority on it. He'd put out another call on Ritter: he didn't think X was Ritter, but he'd like to clear him out of the way if possible. So then, before going home, he called Wilcox Street to see if Ritter had been picked up; and surprisingly he got D'Arcy.

"What are you doing still there?" he asked. It was ten o'clock.

"Overtime," said D'Arcy. "So will you be, boy. Smart M.D. in Boyle Heights handed us two of the bank robbers. Gomez got Curly Hair in one shoulder, they came in with a gun to force the M.D. to treat it, and all very cunning he agreed, locked the outer office door so they wouldn't be interrupted, managed to lock himself into an inner office and called Hollenbeck. So we've got these two, just starting out to question them, so you can come back and join the party."

"Oh, hell," said Maddox. "All right."

But there was Offenbach. Nice and safe in the County Jail. To question in depth.

On the Ruth and Ronnie thing. Offenbach looked quite hot for that, right now.

Eleven

THEY HAD, IN FACT, PICKED UP ALL THREE BANK ROBBERS. When D'Arcy said "them" he wasn't, of course, including Curly Hair, who'd been carted off to the General in an ambulance. There is very seldom a great deal of honor among thieves, and the second man, seeing they'd been dropped on, wasn't about to let the other partner get clean away to enjoy the approximately seven thousand bucks they'd got from the bank; he told them who he was and where to find him—an old hotel on Ivar Avenue—so they went and picked him up with no trouble. He was, as a matter of fact, taking a bath when they walked in.

Curly Hair hadn't any record; the other two did. They got statements from them and booked them in at the new jail facility on Alameda, and went home, leaving the office to the night men. It was always nice to clear one up as quickly as that, and the hospital was now saying the chief teller would be O.K., which was nice too.

And just maybe they'd cleared up the Ruth and Ronnie thing too. Maddox hoped so.

Evidently their practical joker had taken another night off;

nothing showed up in that line on Thursday morning. What did show up was discouraging, but any cop had learned to be philosophical about things like that. They had to.

Maddox was about to go out and look for Ritter when the man from Ballistics called.

"About this gun you wanted a test run on. The S. and W. army revolver."

"Yes?"

"Sorry to tell you it's not the one used on your homicide. Markings don't match at all."

"Oh hell," said Maddox. Offenbach had looked really promising. And you could say, wishful thinking, so he'd had two of the same model, would he have the sense to get rid of the other one? Why should he have? With that arsenal—

So that was the F.B.I.'s baby. Of course, in California you didn't need a license for a gun kept on the premises, but he could scarcely claim he needed all those guns for protection. However, whatever he'd planned to do with them, whoever he'd planned on shooting, it hadn't evidently been Ruth and Ronnie.

"I swear to God," Maddox said to Rodriguez, "this is being a bastard. You'd have thought we'd have got some place on it in five days. The only thing I can figure is that there wasn't any kind of motive, or not much motive, and so it could be anybody. Maybe somebody we haven't even heard of yet."

"I see that," said Rodriguez inattentively, scarcely looking up from *See Them Die.* "That's the tough kind."

"And that is not what you're paid for," said Maddox. He got up. "The hell of it is, the people it *could* be—like Ritter—no evidence one way or the other. I think I'll lean on Ritter a little."

He hadn't much faith in that, but he went downtown and found Ritter at home. He brought him back to the station and he and D'Arcy and Rodriguez started the routine questioning.

Various people were always telling Maddox he was a pessimist by nature, and maybe he was; anyway, he wasn't surprised when Ritter turned out a forlorn hope too. Every lead they'd had on this thing had died a natural death on them. The first obvious theory—an ex-boy friend—hadn't turned up anything. When they'd listened to Ann Wales, Wales had looked like a very hot prospect, and then it turned out he was alibied by a cop; then Offenbach had turned up, and he'd looked good for it too, and then it turned out his S. and W. army revolver wasn't the one that had cooled Ruth and Ronnie. It was damn farfetched to say he'd had two. Ritter had a motive of sorts, on Ruth—and a record; but they couldn't tie him to any gun at all. He went on insisting that he'd come home by midnight that Friday night and gone to bed; he was a tough customer, he knew the ropes, and he wasn't going to be easy to break. It wasn't until nearly noon that they got anything useful, and they wouldn't have got that if a tall sandy-haired fellow named Barton hadn't come asking to see Maddox. Barton was Ritter's parole officer, and he'd been told by a couple of Traffic men about Ritter frequenting bars and his old pals, and consequently Ritter's parole was being revoked, and Barton had come to collect him.

"Manager at his place said you'd picked him up. You've got a charge on him?"

"I don't know," said Maddox. "Suppose we go break the bad news to him. He just may have a little more to say than we've been getting out of him so far."

That Ritter had. After doing some loud swearing at the damned fuzz and the goddamn-fool rules and regulations, he stared at Maddox bitterly and said, "So you come trying to lay a murder rap on me! Right and left I get it, guy's done a little time you don't give him no damn privacy at all, do you? I don't know I swear to God what the P.A. office thinks we are, anyway—not human or something, we done time? So I was out, I wanted stay out, so you come asking about that night, I'm gonna tell you I got a alibi so's you can whistle up the P.A. officer and toss me back to finish the time? So now I get tossed back anyway, goddamn it, so I tell you and you can go to hell, bloodhound."

"I did wonder," said Maddox. "The alibi?"

"I was with a dame. Darlene O'Neill. At her apartment on Roosevelt Avenue. No, she's not a pro. She's clean, and she'll tell you. What the hell, all the damn rules—"

So that looked like being that. "And you know," said Maddox when Barton had taken him out, "he's right in a way about the rules. It's against human nature. A lot of the only friends a fellow like that has are also ex-cons—and after a long dry spell in Quentin, a man's not necessarily a drunkard if he stops in a bar for a few beers. While as for all righteously saying he's got to keep away from the females—" He sighed. "Well, some of these ivory-tower boys do get funny ideas, all right. So now where do we go looking on Ruth and Ronnie?"

"Well, Offenbach's N.G.," said D'Arcy, "but when we first came across him, you said it could be somebody else like that too—ex-boy friend. Talk to some of her best friends."

"Yes. Could be. And her address book—well, all your closest friends don't necessarily get in address books. I think I'll run up and ask the family about that. Oh, and César, call the Welfare office and ask about that Reyes family—where the amorous landlord lives. It just could be."

And that was wild, but the way the thing shaped made it look as if the motive had been very slight. Maddox wasn't thinking now that there'd been no motive at all, because X had deliberately lain in wait there for them to come home from their date—so, not just a nut loose with a gun, no. But nothing whatever had shown up on Ruth or Ronnie to point to a really solid reason for anyone wanting them dead.

He went up to Franklin Avenue and saw Mrs. Evans for the first time, a still pretty, dark woman; but now her face looked ravaged. The only child— Why did these senseless damn things have to happen?

She told him that Ruth's closest friends had been Marjorie Ferguson, Rose Wyatt, Jean Warren. They had all gone to school together. "Not Rose, she didn't go to college, she's married and has a little boy." Her mouth trembled on that and she said irrelevantly, "We l-liked Ronnie so much—ambitious and he'd have—they'd— Excuse me. You—you don't have any idea yet who—"

He told her they were still working it. He only hoped that something would turn up sooner or later, that this wouldn't be one they finally had to give up on for lack of any leads at all. You got those too, and like all cops he hated that sort of thing: he didn't like feeling inadequate.

He stopped at a drugstore for lunch and called in to the office to pass on those names: Wyatt and Ferguson hadn't been in the address book. Other places they hadn't looked: places Ronnie had worked.

The Rayco Cleaners on Western . . . Raymond Correli

looked at his badge and said, "Sure, anything you want to know, but I don't suppose I'd know anything to help you. That's a damn awful thing to happen, young Morgenstern shot like that—and the girl too. Some nut must've— Well, you can see this is just a small place, but there's just me to run it, and it keeps me busy. I'm a widower, live alone, my daughter's married well—M.D. out in Culver City—and it paid me, hire Morgenstern keep my books. I mean, gave me my spare time to myself, 'stead of slaving here all hours. He came in on Saturday afternoons, kept up the books. Good, he was—knew what he was doing, and you could trust him. . . . I never had a cross word with him all the time he worked for me, which was nearly three years. I paid him ten bucks every Saturday, he'd maybe be here two, three hours. My God, Officer, we even agreed on politics, what'd I be arguing with him for?"

"I just asked," said Maddox. "Where were you that Friday night? I'm sorry, Mr. Correli, but this is being a tough one, we've turned up no motive at all and what it comes to, we're asking everybody who knew him."

"Well—" Correli shrugged—"as it happens you can cross me off right away. Friday, you said—yes, yes, I saw about it in the afternoon paper, just as I was wondering why he hadn't showed up that Saturday. I went to my daughter's for dinner that night because it was my grandson's birthday, he was three, and afterward my son-in-law and I got to talking—after the children were in bed, you understand, and I don't usually stay so late, but, well, we got talking and it was about twelve thirty, twelve forty when I left."

Culver City. Well, he could have made it up to Franklin Avenue in time, but that was wild too, because X couldn't have been certain just when they'd come back from the date;

he'd have lain in wait there, probably, from at least ten thirty on.

Maddox went on to the High Hat Tavern on Western Avenue. It was a hole-in-the-wall, scarcely thirty feet long and fifteen wide, a run-down looking little place outside, with—at this hour of the day—a lone customer to keep the bartender company. The bartender, a middle-aged, moon-faced fellow in a very clean white apron, blinked at Maddox and agreed that Morgenstern had come in every Tuesday afternoon and kept the books up to date. The bartender turned out to be the owner; he'd just bought the place and was trying to, he said, smarten it up like. He'd just painted it himself inside, and figured to put on a new front. Stuff like that he could do, but keeping books he hadn't much head for. "Guy I know up the street—at the novelty shop—said this Morgenstern was, you know, trustworthy and all, so I hired him. . . . No, he seemed to be a nice guy, I was shocked as hell when I see in the papers about— Well, I'd never talked much with him, I'd be out here and he'd be in the back room. . . . What the hell you mean, I have any prejudice? Sure I got prejudice—I got prejudice against guys got prejudice, and you're one smart detective not to see the name over the door's Goldstein."

Mr. Goldstein had been in Las Vegas on Friday and Saturday nights, with his wife.

Depressed, Maddox went up the block to the novelty shop. The novelty shop—well, it was a word for it—sold all sorts of things described as "fun-filled." Practical jokes of the crudest sort, plastic snakes, Frankenstein costumes, trick glasses that spilled their contents down your chin when you tried to drink out of them. The merry middle-aged man who ran the place was still terribly shocked over the murder. He'd liked young

137 —

Morgenstern, fine young chap, ambitious, clean-cut, it was just terrible what had happened. No, he'd certainly never had any arguments with him, no cause to, and didn't know anybody else who had. And he quite understood they had to check—on Friday night he'd been at home with his wife and daughter, and there'd been a late movie on TV they all wanted to see, must have been a good one thirty when they got to bed. . . .

Being in the neighborhood, Maddox wandered up the block to Mrs. Barker's house, and found her in her front yard energetically picking dead leaves from the long row of ivy geraniums along the sidewalk. He asked dispirited questions, some of them the same ones he'd asked before; she went on shaking her head. She didn't remember any names of friends Ronnie'd had come to see him, or any more than she'd already told him.

Presently old Mr. Rhys came shuffling up the street, and stopped to say hello to Mrs. Barker. He squinted at Maddox, recognizing him slowly. "You—you found out anything about who—did it yet, Officer?"

Maddox shook his head. Looking at old Mr. Rhys, he felt a sudden cauld grue up the back of his neck: the old man with nothing, nothing, nothing. Dragging out his days alone in the cheap rented room . . . What else, maybe, waited for Ivor Maddox, forty years on? Ought to get married, he thought absently. Some nice girl. Have a family. But—

"Oh." Mr. Rhys blinked at him, his eyes watery and rheumed. "It's just an awful, awful thing. I can't rightly get over it, you know." He shook his head. His shabby tan work pants were stained, one pocket torn; the faded blue shirt he wore had been only half pressed. Nobody to take proper care of the old man. "It don't seem fair," he said. "Ronnie."

"I suppose," said Mrs. Barker heavily, "we just got to have faith and figure God's got some reason, Mr. Rhys."

"I don't know as I could rightly believe," said the old man, "even so. Such a downright good young chap like that. Not fair at all."

"Sometimes things look that way," agreed Maddox unoriginally. He left them there, the old man still shaking his head slowly back and forth, back and forth, staring down unseeingly at the brightly pink-blooming ivy geraniums.

Maddox was feeling more depressed when he trailed into the office at four o'clock. Rodriguez was sitting at his desk eating a sandwich, absorbed in See Them Die.

"That's not—" said Maddox.

"Can't I take ten minutes' break? I never got time for lunch at all. We were just starting out to hit all those names in her address book—D'Arcy went to see the Wyatt and Ferguson girls—and just as I was leaving we got a call. Burglary discovered over on Catalina, people'd been away and just got home. Whole damn place ransacked. So I went out on that with Dabney, and he picked up a lot of latents, only now we've got to eliminate the householders and all their friends, if the prints don't show in Records. Then I went to see this Evelyn Sanders—out of the address book—and she works to hell and gone at a place off the Pomona freeway. I only got back half an hour ago. And then—"

"Oh," said Maddox. "She have anything to offer?"

"Nada. She and Ruth weren't specially close friends, she knew Ruth had dates but not much about them—did know she was engaged. Didn't, she said, especially approve of what she called mixed marriages, she's an Episcopalian, but that was Ruth's affair after all. She hadn't seen her in a couple of months. And—"

"Yes. I've covered all the places he held jobs. Not a smell," said Maddox. "Just nothing. Everybody liked him, or at least didn't dislike him at all, thought he was perfectly honest and trustworthy, was quite satisfied with his work. Well, so D'Arcy went to see those two pals of Ruth's. I wonder what he's got."

"I can tell you what he hasn't got," said Rodriguez, putting down his paperback regretfully and taking the last bite of his sandwich. "I tell you, Ivor, I think it's his timing that's off. He meets that Margaret Talmadge and falls for her just when her mother's been murdered, so naturally she sort of connects him in her mind with that, he reminds her of it—being one of the cops on the case—and she's not going to be very favorably inclined to going out with him. ¡Cómo no! And so now he falls for this—mmh—bouncy little blonde Sandra, so he's out of the office when she comes in. She—"

"She came in?"

"Mmh. About half an hour ago, just as I did. Nobody else here. She's really more my type than D'Arcy's," said Rodriguez reflectively. "Cute, isn't she? I like them cute. D'Arcy wants one more serious, more—you know—mature. But if he'd been here instead of me, ten to one he'd have a date with her now—she likes cops. Quite frank about it." Rodriguez stroked his mustache complacently.

"César, you didn't— All I need is you and D'Arcy feuding with each other over a—"

"Well, no, I didn't," said Rodriguez. "I restrained myself nobly, because I'm pretty sure she'd have jumped at the offer, because I like D'Arcy. But I really can't see him getting any place with that one. He's too serious. Idea of entertaining a girl, sit around and show her his prize pictures—" D'Arcy was a photographer of some talent, his single hobby—"and tell her all about how he decided which f-stop to use." Maddox grinned. "That one, she'll like the bright lights and noisy bands."

"What'd she come in for?"

"Oh, she remembered she hadn't told you the amorous landlord had threatened Ruth with a knife. Threatened to cut her if she wasn't nice to him."

"Oh. You get the address for that place?"

Rodriguez nodded. "Down on Grand Avenue."

"Well, have to look, I suppose. It's not very likely, but—"

"Never know until we look. Do you think—"

Ellis looked in. He said in an annoyed voice, "Me, falling for your little brainstorm! Well, I want to get the guy, but if I'd foreseen what a hell of a wholesale operation it'd turn out to be— Look, will one of you run over and play out the comedy with Carstairs again? Hell, you've both been there before but after all we want to set her up as worth the price, and I guess a satisfied customer could be expected to go back. Ivor—"

"What's the trouble with it?"

"Well, for God's sake," said Ellis, "we've got to make it look plausible if we're going to get anywhere, make Cleveland swallow the bait. And you know bartenders, they just naturally notice things. And like any cocktail bar, that one has regulars coming in, not so many just dropping in once or twice off the street. So we have to plant a man as safeguard for Sue, and send the others in to make like customers, and the bartender isn't going to wonder about all of a sudden all these new faces?

So, to make it look halfway plausible, I tell about half a dozen of them—the uniformed men, and Brougham, and Donny—to make a point, drop in there at odd times, make it look like they're turning into regulars, you take me. Not just to pick up Sue. So now I've got Captain MacDonald screaming I'm undermining the morale, encouraging his men to drink on duty, and I *explain* the setup to him—for God's sake, how can you go into a place like that and maybe order orange juice?—and there's no potted plants to empty drinks into. And he says, Never mind that, we've got rules, he says, and besides he needs all his squad-car men for important business like writing traffic tickets and I've got no business snatching them out of uniform—"

"It's been four days," said Maddox. "Cleveland hasn't shown any interest?"

"That's just it, damn it. Yes, Sue says she's absolutely sure all this, um, activity, has been noticed with interest. And when she stopped at the desk yesterday to ask if there'd been any messages, Cleveland came out of his office and sized her up, made some friendly conversation. He may be working up to propositioning her, and we don't want to rock the boat by having anything look suspicious. At this stage. Right now I've got O'Brien sitting in as safeguard."

"Oh my God," said Maddox and Rodriguez simultaneously. "Would he have the sense to recognize a genuine john?" wondered Maddox.

"But the point is, we can't have a whole parade of new faces wandering in there, to make the bartender curious. I think you'd better start to be a regular too, Ivor. You go over there now, hah, and play little games with Carstairs maybe—satisfied customer back for more."

"Another thing," said Rodriguez, "do we all look the affluent part? Supposedly she's a high-class bit, not the five-buck Main Street lay. Do we—"

"Oh, to hell with that," said Ellis. "This'll have to pay off within the week or not at all. You chase over there, Ivor."

"All right, all right. But I want to hear what D'Arcy got, César—tell him to call me at home if I don't catch him before six."

"Will do."

She was wearing an emerald-green silk sheath this time, just as low-cut and revealing, and Maddox felt the same sense of outrage. The nice girl Carstairs. The funny thing was, of course, he'd have admired the sheath on that seductive wench Sally Scott, or Dulcie, or— But—well, Carstairs was a cop, a good cop, and it was a damned shame she should have to—

Just on account of a couple of unrealistic laws about the nature of evidence in certain vice charges.

She was perched on a bar stool sipping a long drink, the cigarette holder held at an angle. He wondered how she was managing about the drinks, having to sit around here so much. He took the stool next to her, noticing the bartender recognize him, and ordered a Scotch and water. "Hi, Sally."

"Oooh, Johnny," she said, and batted the false eyelashes at him. "Nice to see you again." She gave him a coy smile. And why the hell he'd ever had such a damn fool idea—

O'Brien was sitting over there in the corner studying the shot glass in front of him. Typical, thought Maddox. Order straight rye or Scotch, never considering you couldn't make one drink like that last very long.

They played out the comedy, the heads-together whispers.

She had on the same musky perfume. He let the bartender overhear him. "Hell, girl, that's a price, but I guess maybe you're worth it at that."

She slipped off the stool and went out to the lobby. Maddox sat and finished his drink, went out to the street, into the lobby by the street door, and up to room three twelve. Sue let him in.

"Well, so I'm supposed to be really good," she said dryly. "They're coming back."

"Ellis is running out of men, and afraid to introduce too many new faces," said Maddox. "I did have one hell of an idea, didn't I?"

"You most certainly did," said Policewoman Carstairs. "And carrying this miniature tape recorder inside my bra was not the least of them. It's damned uncomfortable, if you want to know."

"I can imagine," said Maddox meekly. "Er—by the way, how do you manage about the drinks?"

"The— Oh," said Sue. "Corpse Reviver Number Three."

"What? What the hell's that?"

"You don't know it? Quite mild really, and you can make one last practically indefinitely. You take a jigger of Pernod and add some lemon juice and ice cubes and fill the glass with champagne."

"My God," said Maddox.

"Um-hum," said Sue. "One buck twenty-five apiece. I'm an expensive girl, Maddox."

"I hope to God this thing breaks pretty soon, you'll bankrupt us. You look like *hell*," said Maddox. "A respectable L.A.P.D. officer."

"Careful," said Sue. "Just maybe there's a bellhop with his ear to the door."

"And why I had such a harebrained idea—"

"Well, I don't know," said Policewoman Carstairs, "I'm rather enjoying myself, really. Quite fun."

"Fun!" said Maddox, annoyed. "That damn dress—and showing your legs up to—"

"Why, Sergeant, fancy you noticing my legs."

"Yes, well, what does your mother think about it?" asked Maddox angrily. He quite liked Carstairs's mother—nice woman—the once he'd met her.

"Oh," said Sue, drifting over to the mirror, "Mother's terribly amused by it."

Twelve

D'ARCY DIDN'T PHONE, BUT HE SHOWED UP AT THE HOUSE ON Gregory Avenue at a little after seven thirty, just as Maddox had finished dinner. "I don't suppose," he said hopefully, "you'd have a drop of Scotch or bourbon or something around? Technically I'm off duty. I've had a long hard day, with at least one female weeping on my shoulder and a lot of other people to listen to, and I could use a little energizer."

Maddox said, "Left-hand cupboard over the sink, and there're ice cubes in the refrigerator." And, when D'Arcy came back into the living room with a glass in his hand and sank down on the couch, "What did you get?"

"Well, I got something we should have got a few days ago —but it did look so much more likely that the motive went back to one of Ruth's cases, didn't it? Or a thing like Offenbach. I found this Wyatt woman first. Young housewife with a baby, lives out in West Hollywood—husband an insurance man. She told me quite a story—said she'd been so upset all week, since the murder, she didn't know what to do, she didn't want to come in and tell us about it in case it didn't mean anything, and of course it *couldn't* mean anything, but on the other hand it might be—and she didn't know what to do— Women," said D'Arcy. "You can see in a way how she felt. But women I will never quite understand. Cold-blooded logical as you can get about some things, and then other times— But this might just be something, Ivor. About the other girl, this Marjorie Ferguson."

"What about her?"

"Well," D'Arcy stretched out his long legs and took a swallow of his drink, "it's a little involved, but here's the gist of it. Rose Wyatt and the Ferguson girl have been best friends since kindergarten. They both met Ruth in high school and both of them were pretty close friends of hers ever since, but —says Wyatt—she and Marjorie were still closer. From what I sort of gleaned between the lines, because Wyatt was upset and a little incoherent, I gather that Marjorie's always been the weaker party, you get me—tends to lean on people some. All right. It hadn't occurred to us to ask how Ruth met Ronnie, but now we know—Marjorie introduced them. Marjorie had dated him. Marjorie, in fact, was crazy about him."

"Now you don't tell me," said Maddox.

"People knew she'd introduced them, of course. But nobody but Rose knew how Marjorie really felt. About Ronnie, and about him getting engaged to Ruth. It seemed Marjorie met him at a party—home of another girl she knew whose brother's going to L.A.C.C. and brought Ronnie. And Ronnie had asked her out a few times—Rose didn't think very often, and it was just one of those things, apparently he liked Marjorie all right but it was just casual, nothing serious. But it was with Marjorie. She used to come to see Rose and—um— rhapsodize over him—hoped he'd ask her to marry him. He

147 —

was the handsomest, most brilliant and charming fellow she'd ever met, and so on and so forth." D'Arcy swallowed Scotch and water.

"Tell on," said Maddox interestedly.

"Now it seems," said D'Arcy, "that Marjorie Ferguson has had several bad shocks lately. First, her father got killed in a freeway crash last March, and she had—as Rose put it—just adored him, and it was a bad time for her. Her mother too. He didn't leave much, he was chief accountant at a brokerage downtown, but they'd lived up to the hilt of what he made, and the insurance just paid the funeral expenses. Marjorie was working—she was a secretary at the same brokerage—but it meant her younger brother, whom she is likewise very fond of, had to stop college and get a job. Then her mother had a heart attack, and there was a lot of worry about medical expenses. And about the same time Ronnie got engaged to Ruth."

"Yes," said Maddox, "but everybody says he'd been dating Ruth for some time, and nobody else. When he hadn't been hanging around Marjorie, she must have realized he wasn't seriously interested."

"Well, she was in love with the guy," said D'Arcy. "I brought that up, and Rose said of course, but Marjorie just refused to admit it—all starry-eyed, was still hoping he'd wake up and discover she was his own true love. When he and Ruth got engaged, Rose said, Marjorie came to cry on her shoulder. Evidently went all to pieces. Rose was nearly crying on my shoulder at that point, and took about twenty minutes to tell me she didn't for one second believe Marjorie had *meant* it, or could *do* such an awful thing, of course she wouldn't, and when I finally got her calmed down and asked what she meant, she came out—very reluctantly—with this. At that time, Marjorie said she'd want to *die* if Ruth or Ronnie ever suspected how she felt, she really liked Ruth, Ruth was her *friend*—so consequently nobody but Rose ever did know, she kept up the friendship on the surface and never let Ronnie see how she felt. But she said to Rose then, she wished Ruth was dead, she could have killed her for stealing Ronnie. Wishful thinking, sure—if he wasn't seriously interested, he probably never would have been whether he'd met Ruth or not.

"Well, Rose tried to calm her down, make her see reason, accept it, and forget Ronnie. But she says Marjorie couldn't seem to—just kept brooding about it. I gather that she isn't the sort who attracts males in droves—Rose says she's 'quiet' and 'kind of reserved.' "

"I wonder if she was still feeling that way about Ruth," said Maddox.

"Oh, so did I. Continue to listen. I asked Rose. Had she talked about it to Marjorie lately? She got upset again. She said she hadn't known what to *do*, since the murder. It seemed so impossible, *Ruth* getting murdered—and Ronnie, of course. But it was just impossible too that Marjorie— Well, after some more of this I got her down to specifics again, and what it adds up to sounds—" D'Arcy stared into his empty glass and rattled the ice cubes. "The last six months or so, Marjorie's been in a very nervous state, says Rose. All the bad luck in the family, and then Ronnie. And she lost her job about a month ago. Rose didn't know why, Marjorie wouldn't talk about it. When I talked to the brother—the mother was taking a nap, she's still more or less an invalid—it emerged that Marjorie's been having a siege of headaches, various aches and pains—likely what they call psychosomatic—and she'd been off work so much, they finally fired her. I also, after that, talked to her former boss, and he said she'd been efficient enough up to the last few months, when she'd been making a mess of every job she was handed—forgot where papers were, mislaid things, couldn't take a whole letter without asking every word repeated. He tried to be patient, but it just got impossible. He knew what the girl had been through, had known her father, and was sorry for her. He advised her to have a thorough physical checkup, maybe take a little rest, and offered to recommend her for a job when she felt capable again. Well, to get back to Rose. I heard all about Marjorie's nervous state and the job and all, and asked her again if she thought Marjorie was still brooding over Ronnie and Ruth. It was a little like pulling teeth, she didn't want to come right out and say it, but she finally did. When I got her convinced that we don't go railroading people into jail for just any old thing, and wouldn't jump to conclusions. She said—listen to this, now—she said she'd seen Marjorie on Wednesday—week ago yesterday—the latest time she had seen her. Marjorie came to see her that afternoon. She was, said Rose, very low. She was still having these headaches, and she couldn't find another job. She hadn't been to a doctor, wouldn't talk about going. Rose tried to persuade her, told her maybe some vitamins or a prescription of some sort would make all the difference." D'Arcy drained his glass of a little melted ice. "And then she happened to mention that she—Rose, I mean—had seen Ruth the night before, and Marjorie flared up and said don't mention Ruth to her, and then she began to cry. Rose tried to, you know, soothe her down, told her she'd feel a lot better if she'd just accept that Ronnie wasn't for her, she'd find somebody else—you know the line. But Marjorie said to her—just like that—'I wish I was dead, and I wish they were both dead too.' "

"Really," said Maddox. "That's all very interesting. You don't mention seeing Marjorie."

"No, I haven't. She was out job-hunting when I went to where they live—old apartment on Vermont, they had to sell the house after Ferguson was killed—and the brother, whose name is Denis, didn't know when she'd be home, but some time before six. He was worried," said D'Arcy reflectively. "He didn't know I'd got all that from Rose. Well, Rose told me Marjorie hadn't said anything to her family about how she felt, on Ronnie. Naturally. He—the brother—told me he'd been worried about her health, she was terribly nervous lately and she wouldn't go to a doctor. He also said she'd been practically prostrated over the murder. Taking it for granted, because Ruth had been one of her close friends. Said she'd be glad to talk to us, but obviously wouldn't know anything about it."

"I think we go to see Marjorie," said Maddox.

"I figured you'd want to. She'll be home now." D'Arcy set down his glass.

They took D'Arcy's car. "But what kind of setup is it?" said Maddox. "Could she be out of the apartment at one in the morning and the mother and brother not— Oh, I'm not thinking. She'd just have to say she had a date—maybe with a couple of other girls to see a late movie or something, so they wouldn't be surprised at nobody calling for her. . . . Does she use a cigarette holder?"

"I asked. She doesn't smoke."

"Well, nothing says those cigarette butts had to be left by X. And all the trampling around the flower bed there—somebody walking a dog and the dog getting loose and running up there. Or kids. But I rather like Marjorie, D'Arcy. Because it's exactly the kind of irrational motive that isn't any motive that I think triggered it off."

"I had the same feeling."

But they weren't destined to meet and question Marjorie Ferguson that night. When they got to the apartment on Vermont, they found an upset household. Denis Ferguson, an extraordinarily handsome young fellow about twenty-two, was both upset and angry. He didn't ask them why they wanted to question Marjorie beyond saying, "That Ruth Evans thing —yes, Marjorie was one of her best friends but I don't see how she'd know anything about her getting— It's damn thoughtless of her, that's all I say! She knows how Mother worries, and it's bad for her—if she wanted to stay out for dinner, all she had to do was call and say so. She's always home by six, or if she won't be she calls."

Mrs. Ferguson, a thin, ill-looking woman in a housecoat, was more worried than he was. She sat on the couch against cushions, breathing in little gasps, and another middle-aged woman bent over her anxiously. "You're sure you don't need one of your tablets now?"

"No, I'm—all right—but I can't understand where she can be, that's all. Always good—about calling if she plans to be late, and here it is—nearly a quarter to nine. Denis, I keep thinking of an accident."

"Now, Mother, we'd have heard, she's got identification on her." Ferguson turned to Maddox. "I don't know what to do, I'm due at work at eleven, out at Lockheed, but if Marjorie's not home by then I can't leave Mother alone. Mrs. Dewar just came in to be neighborly, I can't— Where the devil is she? Worrying us like this—and," he lowered his voice, "she's been in a funny nervy kind of state lately. Especially this past week. She went all to pieces when she heard about that poor Evans girl—of course to have a thing like that happen to a close friend—" He was looking more worried now. "You don't suppose, my God, she could have lost her memory or something like—"

"Doesn't happen very often, Mr. Ferguson," said Maddox. "Does she have a car? She's driving?"

Ferguson nodded. "Mother's car—Mother's not allowed to drive. It's a fifty-nine Ford two-door— I don't know what the license is."

"It'll be—on that thing—on my key ring," said Mrs. Ferguson faintly.

"Oh yes—just a second, I'll get it." When he came back from the front bedroom, Maddox took down the plate number.

"It's early to put out a call on her," he told Ferguson. "She could simply have got held up somehow, for some reason didn't call. She's an adult, supposedly responsible young woman able to look after herself. Would you know how much money she'd be carrying?"

"Not any more than eight or ten dollars, if that. Are you going to—to put out a call? It's not like Marjorie, it really isn't."

And of course that was what everybody always said who came in to report somebody missing when they were just a couple of hours late home; and nine times out of ten the somebody showed up hale and hearty, full of apologies for having forgotten to call, or having got stalled in a freeway jam, or something like that. But in this case, evidently the girl had been acting a little odd lately, and then there was the fact that she knew her mother shouldn't be worried.

"Would you like us to, Mr. Ferguson?"

"Yes," said Ferguson definitely. "Yes, I would. It's not *like* Marjorie—when she's herself at least. But the way she's been lately—" He stared at them for a moment, looking thunderstruck, and then said, "My God, you don't suppose she *does* know something about that murder? Maybe somebody who had a reason to—and she was nervous about telling, or— But that's fantastic! I thought at the time, when she was carrying on so about it, it must have been a lunatic, because what I'd heard about the girl, there'd be no reason, and Morgenstern sounded like a very upright sort of guy. I just can't see Marjorie— But where the hell is she?"

They got a description, and—from Mrs. Ferguson—a description of the clothes she'd been wearing, and put out a call on both Marjorie and her car. She was five-seven, a hundred and twenty, fair complexion, brown hair, blue eyes, appendectomy scar, no birthmarks, and she'd been wearing a beige cotton shirtmaker dress, tan nylons, a pair of low-heeled brown pumps, carrying a brown leather handbag. Gold Hamilton wristwatch, gold costume earrings, gold costume brooch on the dress, one ring—a U.S.C. seal ring, gold, with her initials on the shank.

A description like that didn't really give you a picture. Maddox looked at the recent snapshot of Marjorie that Ferguson had given him, and silently decided that D'Arcy had been right about her. Looks meant so damn little, good or bad: it was what lay behind, in the person. She wasn't bad-looking, nice enough features, short dark brown hair, a figure rather thin but otherwise not bad. But she wore a sullen, defeated expression, and her shoulders were stooped; she stood grace-lessly facing the camera.

"Good sharp shot," said D'Arcy. "It'll blow up."

They sent out the call, and called it a night. Maddox gave the night desk sergeant at Wilcox Street, Connors, a ring to call him at whatever hour if and when she was picked up.

Considering everything, he liked Marjorie Ferguson. But, he reflected philosophically, he had—at first—liked the idea of an ex-boy-friend of Ruth's, of Ritter, of Wales, of Offenbach.

Now of Marjorie. Who had wished she were dead and that Ruth and Ronnie were dead too.

Hell, he thought. Was that it? Had she maybe driven over to the Pasadena freeway and jumped off the old suicide bridge? Funny how it earned that name—a lot of high places to jump from, if you wanted to, in the county; but the old Arroyo Seco Bridge a favorite spot. Well, when they made up their minds— And, *hell*, if she did—either that way or another way —she'd be beyond questioning, and they'd never know whether she'd somehow obtained the gun and lain in wait there for her own true love and the usurper Ruth to come back from their date. Unless she left a note, of course.

Maddox went to sleep feeling depressed, feeling that this could very well be one where they'd feel morally sure they knew who, but would never get enough evidence to make the charge. Or maybe just never have any glimmer who X had been, period.

The desk sergeant woke him up at two thirty to tell him her car had been found. Routinely checking no-parking zones, a squad car had tagged it, parked in a spot where parking was illegal between midnight and six A.M., and the squad car man

155 —

had spotted the plate number. Nothing in the car but the usual things, maps and a whisk broom, nothing to say where the driver had gone. No keys.

"Where was the car?" asked Maddox sleepily.

"About half a block up from Seventh on Carondelet."

"Oh," said Maddox. "Well, thanks." He put the phone down, still only half awake, and started drifting off to sleep again.

And woke suddenly with a start, and sat bolt upright. He thought, you're losing your grip, boy—an obvious thing like that—

He looked at the clock. For God's sake, five o'clock—just peacefully going back to sleep like that, and his subconscious mind not getting through to him till now.

He dialed rapidly. "Connors? Maddox. Look, you said the car was about at Seventh and Carondelet? That's the Wilshire precinct. Call them and tell them to check MacArthur Park. Right now."

"Oh, for God's sake," said Connors, "and I never thought of it for myself! The obvious— I'll do that and let you know, Sergeant."

Maddox lay down again.

At five forty-five Connors called back and said, "They found her. On one of the park benches by the lake. No, no, she's still alive, but she'd taken something, don't know what. Unconscious. She's at Georgia Street, but unless she's bad or does pass out, they'll probably transfer her to the General. We'll know more later."

"No note?"

"Not by what I got."

"Well, O.K., thanks." There probably wouldn't be any information forthcoming until well along in the morning. Maddox lay down again but didn't go back to sleep.

Was this the answer? He hoped to God they'd save her. Had Marjorie (in her nervous, brooding state, feeling so unloved, unwanted, unlucky—everything happens to me) been the X here? And got to feeling remorseful, or just more depressed—or, as was so often the case with would-be female suicides—they'll be sorry when I'm gone?

Well, have faith in the doctors. And hope.

When he got to Wilcox Street at eight o'clock, feeling stale and pessimistic, D'Arcy was in and had already heard the news. "I called, she's at the General. They pulled her through, doctor said we could probably talk to her this afternoon."

"Well, some good news at least. What'd she taken?"

"About a hundred aspirin tablets. They will try it the hard way. You think she could be our baby? No gun—of course we haven't been over the apartment."

"She could be," said Maddox absently. He was reading the note left on his desk by Joe Rowan, and suddenly began to laugh. "I do like this bird's sense of humor," he said. "Turnabout is fair play."

"What?" said Rodriguez, wandering in. "What bird?" He was carrying a paperback copy of *The Con Man*.

"Our practical joker," said Maddox. "As long as we've got to put off questioning Marjorie, let's go see Mr. and Mrs. Duncan."

The neighbors on Poinsettia Drive (of course, of course, the same general area, only about six blocks from Higman

Street) could and did tell them about Mr. and Mrs. Duncan. Nice enough young people, but just thoughtless and, well, young. Young people, said Mr. Kingsbury who lived on one side of the Duncan house, had so damn much energy. Sure, Duncan had a job—worked as a bookkeeper, some oil company downtown; she didn't—pretty little thing, they didn't mean any harm, but they just didn't realize. After all, said Mr. Kingsbury, some people needed their sleep.

The Hamblens, on the other side of the Duncans, and the Stewarts next to the Hamblens, weren't so charitable. Up to all hours, they said, and noisy! Parties. Phonograph going half the night, sometimes dancing, people talking loud, singing, laughing, all hours—and cars parked solid up the block. Up to one and two in the morning, especially Friday and Saturday nights, but others too. The Duncans hadn't lived there long, maybe six months, and this was a nice quiet neighborhood, folks had hesitated to speak up, maybe start a feud some sort. But it was annoying. Hear them half a block away.

No, nobody could honestly claim the Duncans gave wild parties—maybe one reason neighbors had hesitated to complain. Not the kind of thing where there was a lot of drinking, or fights—like that. No. They were just noisy parties, and lots of parties—just people, the phonograph, keeping people awake. Young people having a good time, drinking a little beer maybe, and being noisy.

Somebody—and it could have been one of the neighbors, but considering the care and planning involved (as well as the money) Maddox was convinced it was their practical joker— somebody had taken steps to reinforce the few mild protests neighbors had made to the thoughtless young Duncans.

And now they knew why the practical joker had taken the preceding night off.

James and Carolyn Duncan belonged to a square-dancing club. Every Thursday night they went out square-dancing, got home at about one thirty A.M., and so every Thursday night was peaceful along that block, the young Duncans reveling elsewhere.

But that night hadn't been exactly peaceful for the young Duncans. While they were out square-dancing, somebody—the practical joker who so unaccountably knew so much about the personal foibles of so many different people—had got into the Duncan house. (Rowan's note said, "Adding insult to injury, keep them up asking questions—you can—no idea if any doors left unlocked.") There was, in the young Duncans' bedroom, a double bed with an electrical outlet in the wall behind the headboard. The practical joker had put under the double bed no less than fifteen small electric alarm clocks—it was a double outlet but he'd needed several extension cords to accommodate them all—timed most diabolically to go off at three A.M., three one A.M., three two A.M.—

The thoughtless young Duncans had, in fact, had a taste of their own medicine. Just as they'd got soundly asleep— And it would probably have taken them, swearing and sleepy, some time to locate the origin of the noise—

"Just retribution," said Maddox. "I'm really beginning to like this fellow. *Electric* alarm clocks—of course, so that the ticking wouldn't alert them—and they'd be at least four or five bucks apiece. And how the hell did he know there was an outlet handy enough that the wires wouldn't show? You know, I do like this boy—what a devilishly appropriate—"

Thirteen

THEY FOUND CAROLYN DUNCAN READY TO LAUGH AT THE JOKE
quite as merrily as anybody else. "You should have heard Jim
swear—we'd only just got to sleep really—and we couldn't
imagine *what*—" She giggled. She was a very pretty little
blonde. "Well, I guess maybe we just didn't realize how we'd
been bothering people. A lot of people around here are middle-aged, you know, and— Oh, Jim was mad but when he
calmed down he did see the joke." She grinned ruefully. "Now
I stop to think, Mrs. Kingsbury was polite about complaining,
and we didn't realize—"

"Would you have any guesses as to who might have done
it?" asked Maddox.

She shook her head. "I suppose one of the neighbors, but
honestly I can't see any of them—the ones I know are awfully
—awfully *staid*."

"How did he get in? Was a door or window forced?"

"I guess by the back door," said Mrs. Duncan with another
ingenuous giggle. "Half the time I forget to lock it, I did last
night."

"Well. You know anyone named Endler?—or Foster?—
Rasmussen?—Burdick? You don't. Well, thanks very much."

"If you find who did it—well, you wouldn't arrest them or

anything? It was just a joke," said young Mrs. Duncan. "We wouldn't want you to arrest them. The man who came last night took all the clocks away with him."

For Dabney to print. And find nothing but smudges. "Now who in God's name knows about all these people?" said Maddox exasperatedly. "None of them know each other, a couple of the places are nearly a mile apart if in the same general area, and—"

"We ought to make a little effort to get him," said D'Arcy, "the way the papers are using it to make fun of us." After the pig, a couple of astute reporters had also surmised there'd be more to come, and hung around to find out. The carton of cleanser and the works of Freud for the fanatic housekeeper were a bit subtle and might carry implications of libel, as did the Rasmussen thing, but the skeleton had received a little spread, and the accompanying story poked a little solemn fun at the boys in blue out hunting the joker.

"Well, I've got no ideas on it at all," said Maddox. "After that Packard-Bell link fell through— I wonder if they'd let us see Marjorie now."

"I haven't heard about Marjorie," said Rodriguez. "Have we got a new lead?"

Maddox and D'Arcy told him about Marjorie. "Neurotic female," he said thoughtfully, "sounds good for it. One thing it'd explain, the wholesale fusillade. She wouldn't be familiar with guns and she wanted to make sure of them both, so she fired a couple of rounds."

"And against that," said Maddox, "I'll point out that although she wouldn't be experienced with guns, if it was her she managed to find out damn quick how to reload in a hurry, in the dark."

"True."

They went back to Wilcox Avenue and Maddox called the General. "Yes, you can see her," said the doctor he talked to. "I don't know how much it'll be worth to you, though. Her brother's here. Well, she's in a very disturbed state, I really couldn't— I'm neither a cop nor a psychiatrist, just a hardworking intern, Sergeant, and I think I'll leave it to you and/or a head doctor to say whether she's lying, or legally nuts, or what. Maybe you'll have a guess when you've seen her."

Maddox ruminated and thought he'd see Marjorie alone. Rodriguez was snatching a few minutes to get on with *The Con Man.* D'Arcy said suddenly, "Could it be a domestic?"

"Who?"

"The joker. No, I didn't mean that—what suddenly came to me is, somebody like a domestic, woman who does odd jobs part time, baby-sitting, cleaning—somebody like that would likely know all this about these people. And she might have gossiped about it and been overheard by our joker."

"A little farfetched," said Maddox.

"I don't think so. I'd like to call around, find out if any of them had hired the same person."

And there really wasn't anywhere else to send either of them to look, on Ruth and Ronnie—the more important business—so Maddox shrugged. He said he'd go to see Marjorie, and as he got up Dabney looked in.

"Thought I'd cheer your morning with some good news," he said. "I got four nice clear dabs off one of those clocks. He slipped up. That particular clock, I found when I came to examine it, it's got a very sticky alarm setter. Have to put out all your strength to move the thing, and I can see how he came to be absentminded and leave the latents. He probably tried moving it with one hand and then the other—sometimes you can get a better purchase left-handed—gloves hampered him and he took them off. He may have been in a hurry, or he may have just forgotten to wipe the body of the clock when he'd got the alarm set. Anyway, there they were. Nice and clear."

"Hurray, hurray," said D'Arcy. "And if they don't turn out to belong to the salesman who sold the clock, are they going to show up in anybody's records?" That, of course, was the little catch about fingerprints: absolutely no use all by themselves. "I really don't think the joker has a pedigree downtown."

"Well, it's odds on he did some time in one of the services. Anyway, I sent them downtown and also back to Washington, so we should hear eventually, one way or the other."

"I'd still like to make those calls," said D'Arcy.

Maddox told him to go ahead, and went out. As he passed the desk downstairs, Carter was asking crisp, terse questions on the phone; he raised a hand at Maddox, and Maddox paused. "O.K., there'll be somebody on it. . . . Looks like a suicide, Sergeant—just reported. That was Finch. Woman, her sister just walked in and found her. Finch says an educated guess is she's been dead a couple of days. You want to take it?"

"Pass it upstairs," said Maddox. "I'll see what it looks like later." Right now, Marjorie looked a little more important to him than a dead woman.

He talked with Denis Ferguson in the quiet corridor outside the soundproofed rooms in the psychiatric ward. Ferguson was looking dazed, completely bewildered and incredulous. He said he just couldn't believe it, and just couldn't understand it. He said, "You read about things like this, you never think it could happen in your own family. I don't understand how— My God, my God, what this'll do to Mother—" He was red-eyed, grim. "When the police called and told me, I couldn't—I didn't *believe* it, but just sort of automatically I told Mother—an accident, and Marjorie'd be all right—but now, my God, I don't know. How did all this happen?" He dropped his head into his hands, and then looked up again at Maddox. "I—I thought I knew a little about people. Now I'm not so sure. So I don't know. I don't know—what you, or a psychiatrist, or a—or a judge would— But it's ridiculous! She couldn't have—she couldn't have done th-that." He stopped short, and very carefully lit a cigarette. "Please—you realize she's—upset? I don't—"

From all that, Maddox wasn't too surprised by Marjorie. There was a nurse with her, and she was sitting up in bed in the plain outsize hospital gown, her hair combed but hanging limp around her face, no make-up on. She was perfectly quiet, sipping at a glass of milk, and she looked at Maddox with a tense, anxious expression, looked at his badge, and said, "I knew you'd come. I was expecting you. You don't have to ask me any questions, I'll tell you."

"Miss Ferguson, you know it's your privilege to have a legal representative here while I question you? Do you want that?"

"A lawyer, you mean. I don't want a lawyer," she said. She wasn't paying any attention to the nurse. "I don't *deserve* a lawyer. I want to tell you about it. I've got to tell somebody. That doctor—*he* didn't know, he *said* he was a psychiatrist but he didn't *know*. He laughed at me and said—and said the mind is a lot tougher than most people think. But I'm *not* all right, and I'm not going to be all right, I've suspected it for months and I was afraid but I was afraid to tell, afraid to say it right out." She had a thin shallow voice and she was talking compulsively, agitatedly—"I'm going crazy, I'm going out of my mind! I know it. I've known it. I do things and forget I've done them, and I forget to do the most ordinary things, and all these terrible headaches, I can't think any more, do you understand that? I get just too tired to think— the pain—and I go and do things without knowing I'm doing them at all, and that's how I know. Please, I never meant to do such a terrible, terrible thing—it's not a thing the real me could ever do, you've got to understand that, but I just wasn't myself when I did it, because I don't remember it at all. It's like—it's like some evil spirit's taken possession of me, the way people used to believe." She began to sob, and put down the glass of milk, but after a moment she stopped, and took several long breaths, and began to talk again. "I was so—I was so— Ruth was my friend but I couldn't bear, I just couldn't bear—them together—like that—thinking of them together. I said that about wishing she was—was—but I didn't really, I didn't think I did—not really. And I don't remember but I know I must have—it was me, I did it, it was me, because nobody else at all would have had any reason to. Do you see? I expect you've found that out," and that sounded dreary. "Ronnie—Ronnie—everybody liked Ronnie. And Ruth—nobody but me would have— And with my mind going like this —how I could do such a terrible thing and not even remember it—and I thought, I tried to think—through the headaches— and I couldn't, I couldn't tell and have it all come out—whatever you did to me for it. Mother, and Denny going with that nice Driscoll girl, she'd think— I couldn't, so in the end I thought—I thought I'd just d-do it myself and people would wonder but it wouldn't be so terrible as if it all came out, for Mother and Denny." She looked at him piteously and swallowed. "Do you see? And I hadn't—hadn't anything like sleeping pills, but I'd read somewhere once that enough aspirin—so I— And then it wasn't any good after all." Her face crumpled and she began to cry.

"You're telling me that you shot Ruth Evans and Ronald Morgenstern?" asked Maddox formally.

"Yes. Yes, it was me. It must've been me, because nobody else— But I wasn't in my right mind. Any real psychiatrist would know that and tell you," she said earnestly. "I don't remember doing it, and I don't know where I got the gun or what I did with it afterward. I'm sorry, I'm sorry. I was crazy —because why would I shoot Ronnie? Oh, Ronnie—Ronnie—" She was weeping in a weak helpless way. "The person—the person I used to be'd never—but now I don't know what I'm doing, my mind—"

Maddox looked at her in silence for a long minute. Then he asked, "Miss Ferguson. Have you recently found any money missing from your bag—or bank account—that you couldn't account for?"

"Oh, I thought of that," she said, blowing her nose, wiping her eyes. "The gun, you mean. I don't know anything about guns, the—the person used to be me, really. No, I hadn't. But what it is, sometimes I just don't know what I'm doing, and so I know—I know— Oh, I was so frightened, I didn't know what to do, I—"

"Yes, you've been through a bad time," said Maddox, "but I think you'll be all right now, Miss Ferguson. You just listen to what the doctors say." He wasn't any psychiatrist either, but his guess would be that she was entirely sane; she'd been reasoning logically in a way, if on a false premise.

"All *right?* When I'm— You're not going to—" She looked at him wildly.

"Now, dear, don't get upset," said the nurse.

"Upset!" said Marjorie. "I'm going insane and I must have murdered two people and you tell me not to get *upset!* I've tried to tell you how it's been—please—"

She was still talking when Maddox went out. Denis Ferguson was standing a little way down the corridor, with a very tall elderly man; he was looking very relieved, and he beckoned to Maddox.

"This is Doctor MacDougal—if you'd listen to what he— Sergeant, you can't really believe it, it's fantastic that she—"

"What's your opinion, Doctor?" Maddox looked at MacDougal interestedly. He was a vigorous-looking man at least seventy, with an untidy shock of gray hair, a wide humorous mouth, and a pair of the bluest and sanest eyes Maddox had ever seen.

"Well, sir—you'll be police, and by the look of you not one to go jumping to conclusions. Miss Ferguson is rather interesting, poor girl. Of course I've not carried out all the tests I want to—I'd like to do an encephalogram, of course, and a blood test among others. But I may say I'm not without experience—and a modicum of common sense," and his eyes twinkled briefly. "I should doubt very seriously that Miss Ferguson's committed any murders—er—?"

"Sergeant Maddox. Yes, so do I," said Maddox. "What do you think about all this losing-my-mind bit?"

MacDougal sniffed thoughtfully. "The more we find out

about the mind," he said, "the more we discover how seldom any trouble is really caused by the traumatic shocks or childhood fears or—ah—all that jazz, as my grandson would put it, and how often it is a purely physical thing. I'd give a shrewd guess that we're going to find, one," he raised a bony forefinger, "that Miss Ferguson has at least secondary anemia, and two, a bad sinus congestion. Have either of you ever suffered a sinus headache?" Maddox and Ferguson shook their heads. "The pain can be extremely intense—extremely. To the point, over a period of time, if no alleviating medication is taken, of some mental disorientation. I understand Miss Ferguson's refused to see a doctor."

"Yes," said Ferguson. He looked serious. "God, if she thought she was going crazy—the poor kid, all because—"

"I also understand, from what you've told me, that she's been going through a sad time emotionally—your parents—Um, yes. That didn't help. It's no great wonder. Barring any surprise we may get from the encephalogram—and I really think we'll find the results quite normal—I'd say that immediate treatment for the anemia, and something to relieve the sinus congestion, should see her back to normal in short order. The anemia, of course, is what's caused the intense depression."

"That's—my God, and to think I—" Ferguson let out a great sigh. "You don't know how you've relieved me, Doctor. God, it seemed as if everything going wrong—"

MacDougal touched his arm. "We all go through bad patches. Sometimes, even as a supposed scientist, I think it must be in our stars. I think she'll be all right." He smiled at Maddox and started back down the corridor.

"You aren't thinking—" said Ferguson.

"No, I don't think I am," said Maddox. He contemplated the brown composition floor. "Tell me. Marjorie, so far as you know, was home that Friday night."

"I'm on the night shift. I wasn't there. She was there when I left at ten thirty, sure. And I'll say this," said Ferguson steadily. "She and Mother share a room, you know, and Mother's a very light sleeper like most invalids. I'm morally sure she'd have waked up if Marjorie had gone out."

"Yes. We do have to be thorough and go through the tiresome routine," said Maddox. "We'll have a look through the apartment—for that gun—but it's about a million to one it's there. I think you're very lucky—your sister most of all—that that wise old bird," he nodded after MacDougal, "got assigned to her. He's probably right."

"God, I hope so," said Ferguson. "Talk about nightmares! Marjorie, confessing a— I never dreamed she was so crazy in love with that fellow—poor kid."

"This may have cured her," said Maddox soberly.

On the way back to Wilcox Street, he thought that maybe there was something to be got on Ronnie at the college. Just possibly? César had talked to all his instructors, he'd said; but that had been on a Saturday. There were some Saturday classes, as there were night classes; that college catered chiefly to the working students. Maybe somebody who had been in one of Ronnie's classes knew something?

Argument with another student? Over what? Somebody stealing his notes? For God's sake. And it was outside Ruth's house they'd been—

He parked the Frazer-Nash, walked into the precinct house —casting one glance up the block at the handsome new concrete-and-glass-brick County Health Building. Not even a coat of paint for the precinct house. Naturally. Who cared about cops, where they worked with what equipment?

He wondered why he'd ever wanted to be a cop.

He climbed the stairs. Ellis's office was empty. He met Sergeant Daisy Hoffman in the hall and she smiled at him as she passed. He went into the office. Rodriguez was typing up a report, swearing in Spanish when the keys jammed; *The Con Man* sat open, face down, on his desk. D'Arcy was absent.

"I swear to God—" began Maddox, and the phone rang on his desk; he picked it up. "Maddox."

"Oh, Ivor." Dulcet female voice. Who? "Ivor darling, have you been hibernating or something? I haven't seen you in ages —well, at least three weeks." That redhead, Sheila Farrell. "I'm having a party tomorrow night, dear, you can come, can't you? Rather spur of the moment, but you *must*."

"Well, I don't know," said Maddox. It was a little problem. The cross he had to bear, and as Brougham said, How career-minded could you get? No Trappist monk, but he did mean to make more rank, and all the rules and regulations—

"Please, Ivor! Darling, I *do* want you, don't say you've got a date?"

"No, but—" And the funny thing about it was (well, just the way he was built, people came all sorts) he didn't feel at all flattered, all these females chasing him. He'd never know why they did. It got damn boring after a while. It even annoyed him. He supposed, vaguely, because by all the rules he was supposed to be the one to do the chasing.

"Then you *will*. Seven, darling. For dinner. Just a few of us—that Adams man you liked, and— And not a *late* party, dear, and you can stay on after."

"Well," said Maddox. He put the phone down. He thought about Sheila. And Sally. And Dulcie. And several others. All interesting females, but it did get a little damn boring. He wondered briefly why he'd been given the cross to bear, and as usual came to no conclusion. He sat down at his desk and said, "I swear to God, César, in all the ten years I've been a cop—well, only seven since I made rank—I never knew such a case! There's nothing, absolutely nothing on it. It makes no sense. And I never worked on a thing either where we got so many possible leads that fizzled out almost as soon as they turned up. Just look at it! We hear about Ritter, and that looks good—he had a reason to resent Ruth at least. So he's got an alibi. Then we find out about Wales, and he looks even better—so he turns out to have an alibi too. Then Ed Williams hands us that Offenbach, on Ronnie, and he looks very good—my good Christ, he's even got the same model gun that did the job!—so it turns out it's not the right gun. And then D'Arcy turns up this Ferguson girl, and she looks tailor-made for it, so now she's another false alarm. I never knew such a damn case."

"She's N.G.?" said Rodriguez.

"Oh, but absolutely. Hell and damnation. I don't think anybody shot Ruth and Ronnie. I don't think they're dead, because nobody could have shot them. Where haven't we looked, tell me."

"All the ex-boy-friends. All the ex-girl-friends."

"Talk about forlorn hopes. What did the suicide look like?" asked Maddox abruptly.

"Routine. Elsa Klein, thirty-nine, divorcée, lived alone. Sister gave us the breakdown—read between the lines, no harm in the woman, she liked the fun times and the parties, liked the men—full of life. Husband—former—kind of the puritanical type. He divorced her, and got custody of the two kids. Sister says she was all broken up about that—loved the kids, and also thought her husband was too strict with them. Anyway, she'd tried to get at least visitation rights, and the case came up last Tuesday and the bench said No. Because the husband could show—" Rodriguez grimaced—"she'd entertained at least one boy friend overnight. After the divorce, incidentally. Sister said Elsa had been brooding about it, she'd been worried about Elsa. So she goes to see her this morning, she has a key to the apartment, and finds her dead in bed. Sleeping pills. The usual bit—a note, despondent, doesn't want to go on. I do sometimes wonder," said Rodriguez cynically, "if the bench will ever admit the existence of human nature. ¡Por supuesto que no!"

Yes, the rules and regulations, thought Maddox wryly. So often totally oblivious to the rules and regulations of nature, and riding so damn roughshod over the individual personality.

D'Arcy came in looking annoyed. "I thought for a while I had something," he said. "Showed up that both Mrs. Foster and Mrs. Burdick had hired this same woman to help at parties—serve and wash dishes, you know. One Mabel Kling. But none of the rest of 'em the joker's visited ever heard of her. Dead end. And Mrs. Foster and Mrs. Burdick had never hired any other domestic. Damn all, in fact. I just can't— What'd you get out of Marjorie?"

"Damn all," said Maddox. "I never knew such a case. Every single lead we—"

"Well, you've broken one, Sergeant," said Dabney from the door. He came in, holding a yellow teletype in one hand, looking amused. "You can go pick up your practical joker. Washington was very prompt and obliging—came up with this just now. Make on the prints."

"What, for God's sake, you don't mean—"

"I do mean to say. The Feds had his prints because he was in Civil Service."

"In Civil—" Maddox sat up. "What the hell—"

"I hope you don't mind," said Dabney apologetically. "I was interested in this one—you might say, such really practical practical jokes, trying to get people to see their own shortcomings. I checked it out myself, Sergeant, when I got the teletype. He was a Post Office employee. Henry George Kindler. Worked for the Post Office for thirty years, retired last May. Before retirement age—he's only fifty-three. They gave me the branch—the Hollywood Post Office. So I called there. Seems he retired because he got a big legacy from an old uncle— fellow I talked to said nearly half a million. Said it couldn't happen to a nicer guy, everybody likes Henry. He's a widower, lives alone. And, see, he had that route, the supervisor said— that route that takes in where all those people live that had the jokes played on them. He had it for nearly twelve years, and he's the friendly sort, talks to everybody, and they talk to him. So he'd naturally have got to know—people knowing him, and coming out with the casual talk—you can see—"

"The *mailman?*" said D'Arcy. "For God's sake, we never thought of the *mailman.*"

Fourteen

HENRY GEORGE KINDLER, THE JOLLY EX-MAILMAN, LIVED AT an address out on Rosewood Avenue. At the moment, they hadn't much else on hand except, of course, Ruth and Ronnie, and they were all curious about Kindler; they all got up to go and see him. And a tall, dark, good-looking man in his forties stepped into the office and said, "Is this— I'm looking for a Sergeant Maddox. The sergeant downstairs said—"

"Yes sir, I'm Maddox. What can I do for you?"

"I'm Martin Rasmussen," said the man.

"Oh yes, sir. Sit down. What—"

"Well, I came in to ask you—to tell you—" Rasmussen looked a little embarrassed; looked rueful. "It seems from a couple of things I saw in the paper, whoever—you know— fixed up that booby trap for me has played a few other little jokes."

"Yes," said Maddox. "As a matter of fact, Mr. Rasmussen, we've just found out who it was and were going to pick him up."

"Oh really. Who was it?" asked Rasmussen with intense curiosity. "I couldn't think—"

"It was your former mailman. Henry Kindler."

"Mr. *Kindler?*" exclaimed Rasmussen in naked astonishment. He sat down in the chair beside Maddox's desk and after a moment he said, "Well, I see. Yes. This just—makes me feel all the more so. I—"

"We don't think he meant you to be hurt at all, sir."

"Of course he didn't, if it was Kindler. And *that*— Yet in a way I can see it. Yes. Look, Sergeant. It was just an accident. I don't want to—to charge him with anything. That's what I came in to say. You know, it sort of made me think—lying there in the hospital. All my wife says, and— I suppose you gathered the—the reason for—" He looked more embarrassed, and angry at himself. "Well, I guess the long and short of it is, Sergeant, the whole thing did make me think, and I'm going to turn over a new leaf—or try my damnedest, anyway." He smiled sheepishly. "Hell, I don't want the kids thinking I'm some kind of ogre. . . . *Kindler!* If that doesn't slay me. Really. And yet— Well, I certainly wouldn't want to charge him with anything. You don't have to, do you?"

"Well, Mr. Rasmussen, technically it was assault—"

"Oh for God's sake, assault hell. He'd never have—he didn't mean—"

"But if you don't want to press charges, well," and Maddox shrugged.

"Good. I don't. *Kindler,* of all people. Well, maybe he did me a good turn. You aren't going to do anything to him for the other—"

"The assault was the only serious count," said Maddox. "I don't know how the other victims will feel about charging malicious mischief." Which was all they had on him, of course.

Rasmussen laughed. "Nobody'll want you to charge him

with anything, Sergeant. *Kindler*, my God. Why, he was on that route for years, nice fellow, always cheerful. We all heard about his legacy—" He shook his head and got up. "I can't get over it. But I'm damn relieved he won't get into trouble over it." He hesitated, grinned, and said, "You tell him that —that maybe it straightened me out a little."

"I'll do that," said Maddox. "Good luck, Mr. Rasmussen. . . . So now we haven't got a charge," he added to D'Arcy and Rodriguez. "Unless we want to make it malicious mischief and see him put on probation and fined fifty bucks."

"There's breaking and entering at the Duncans'," said D'Arcy.

"Not breaking. The door was unlocked."

"So it was. Well, I'm damn curious to meet him anyway," said D'Arcy. "I'd like to know where the hell he got the skeleton."

"Which reminds me, by the way," said Rodriguez, "Dabney wants to know what the hell to do with it. Put it out with the trash and scare the refuse collectors, or what? He says it makes Boyce nervous sitting propped up in the corner."

"We'll ask Mr. Kindler if he wants it back," said Maddox. "Come on. I want to know how he got all those bottles across the Fosters' drive, and how he knew there was an outlet under the Duncans' bed."

It was a large old sprawling house, that rarity in southern California, a two-story house with an attic. It had a deep front porch, neatly tended flower beds in front, a neat green lawn, and it had been newly painted spanking white with green trim. A man was sitting on the front porch reading the morning

— 176

Times, smoking a pipe, and rocking gently in his old wooden rocking chair newly painted green.

Maddox, D'Arcy, and Rodriguez went up the front walk and climbed the steps to the porch. "Mr. Henry Kindler?" said Maddox.

"Yes sirs, and what can I do for you?" Kindler smiled up at them innocently. He was a spare man, with a humorous, alert-looking face like a terrier, thought Maddox: a man who'd always been tremendously interested in life and in people, and always would be. A friendly man. Evidently his legacy hadn't prompted him to a grander style of living: he'd just fixed up the place he had.

Maddox brought out his badge and introduced himself, D'Arcy, and Rodriguez. "Oh, police, eh?" said Kindler placidly. "Now what do you want of me, Sergeant?"

"You mind if we sit down?" Maddox sat in the straight chair beside Kindler's, and D'Arcy and Rodriguez took the glider, which creaked a little. "Now, you know, Mr. Kindler," said Maddox gently, "you really shouldn't have got up to all those antics. You really shouldn't. The pink pig, and so on." Remembering the pig, he tried to keep his mouth straight. "In the first place—"

Kindler took the pipe out of his mouth and started laughing. It was honest laughter; he said, "My God, didn't that old sow look ridiculous, though! I suppose it was that one clock. I remembered afterward I'd forgotten to wipe it off after I set it. I'm sorry about this, I'd thought up some real dillies to start working on. But—"

"Where in hell did you get that skeleton?" blurted D'Arcy curiously.

Kindler began to laugh again. "Oh my, old Bart would have enjoyed that one! Nice old fellow, he was, and it used to make me a little mad, how Mrs. Burdick treated him. I'll tell you, boys, it was the skeleton that sort of started it all. You see, my late wife, her father was a doctor, and being kind of old-fashioned, he'd used to have that skeleton in his office when he started practice as a young man, and he'd always hung on to it. Well, he came to live with us after he retired—the boy was grown then, I've got a boy in the regular army, career man, captain now—and he fetched along all his bits and pieces, and upshot was I guess that old skeleton's been sitting around up there in the attic a good ten years. I never gave it a thought till I was up there one day and— Well, I've been having a damn lot of fun with all this money," said Kindler, looking pleased and happy. "An awful lot you can do with money—that fund to send poor kids to camp, things like that, sure, but I really think a person can do more with private charity, you know. I saw that Jimmy Reilly down the street got the money to have his teeth straightened—mother's a widow—and I lent a young fellow money for college, and different things like that. It's been a lot of pleasure to me." Yes, he'd be that kind of man, all right. "I never had much yearning to live in any grand way, but of course I've spent some on myself too—had the house painted inside and out, and bought some new furniture, and hired a gardener to mow the lawn. Well, how it all started—since you've found out it was me and if I'm not boring you—"

"Not a bit," Maddox assured him.

"Well, it was after I got myself a new sofa. A bigger one. I kind of like to stretch out and relax while I'm watching TV.

I thought she'd be easier to shove around, for vacuuming and like that—I've got a woman comes in once a week—if I put some castors on her, and I thought I recalled seeing a set somewhere up in the attic. That was about three weeks ago. So up I goes to have a hunt for them. Found 'em all right, and I was looking around thinking what a lot of stuff you do accumulate over the years, when I saw that old skeleton. I'd forgotten it was there. But I looked at it, you know, and I'd been thinking about old Bart Beckwith, some reason—he was a character, nice old chap—and all of a sudden, maybe I've just got a childish mind—" Kindler twinkled—"I thought what a *hell* of a shock that Burdick woman'd get if some morning she looked out and saw it sitting there in old Bart's chair with his plaid shawl and hat and all. And I just couldn't resist it. I tell you. But once the idea got in my head, give you my word, by the time I brought the thing downstairs and started figuring ways 'n' means, I'd had about half a dozen other bright ideas of the same sort. About people along my old route. I walked that route a good long time, and I like people, getting to know them, and you can't help picking up this and that, if you take me. There was that Clyde Endler, I'd heard the wife a few times going on about his drinking, and that tavern on Sunset where he was going was on my route too, I knew the owner, and he said it was just that Endler'd got into some bad company and was weak. And that Mrs. Foster—well, I don't suppose anything cures that kind, but—" He laughed. "I felt sorry for Mrs. Rasmussen and the kids—heard him railing at the kids Saturday afternoons when he'd be home and I was delivering. Kids, you've got to make allowances. I—"

"If it's any satisfaction to you," said Maddox, "Mr. Rasmussen doesn't want to press charges, for the concussion. He says, in fact, it made him stop and think, and he's going to turn over a new leaf."

"Now, you don't tell me!" said Kindler. "That does make me very happy, Sergeant. Feel I've accomplished something. I didn't know those young Duncans so well, they'd only just moved in before I resigned the job, but I'd heard enough about 'em from the neighbors. She seemed like a nice young thing, just a bit thoughtless. . . . Oh, the outlet under the bed? Well, naturally, I went and looked, couple of nights before I planted the clocks—understood they were careless about locking doors, and I just waited till they went out someplace. Well, you know, I got to thinking—at the very start—sometimes you can sort of make a point to somebody by making 'em laugh about it. Or—well, do you get what I mean? About Mr. Rasmussen—I was sorry he got hurt by it, I never meant that. I just thought, you startle somebody—something like that pig—*didn't* she look damn silly, though!—and sometimes it makes 'em sort of stop and think twice. And anyway, after I had that idea about Dad's old skeleton, it was just too much to *resist*," said Kindler earnestly.

Maddox suddenly had a vision of that skeleton sitting jauntily in its chair holding the newspaper, and began to laugh. "An idea you can say," he gasped. "You've—you've got quite an imagination, Mr. Kindler. Say it twice. That pig—"

"It didn't hurt her, it was only vegetable dye. And I paid for her fair and square, too."

"Yes, we know that." Maddox was still laughing.

"But I promise you, it was quite a job. You ever tried to paint a pig? I had to wait for the pink to dry before I put on the polka dots."

D'Arcy and Rodriguez, remembering the pink pig, began to laugh helplessly.

"Did it in the garage. Awful damn job," said Kindler. "She'd follow if you put a rope on her—that's how I got her in the back of the pickup truck, up the ramp."

"We figured you had one."

"Yep. Figured I'd need one, pull all this—picked it up secondhand. And you know, boys, that pig, I guess it did kind of reach Clyde Endler. I dropped by and sounded out that tavern owner, and he said Endler hasn't been in so often."

"How on earth," said Maddox, "did you get all those bottles of cleanser?"

"Oh, that was a little job too. Sure. I picked 'em up one by one here and there, and then I went by this big supermarket one night—I know the nights they put out their refuse—and naturally they order by the gross and I found the empty carton sitting there to be hauled off. Balanced her on a dolly and up the ramp into the truck. Yes, a little job—but the Fosters' drive is on the side away from the bedrooms. I was quiet even so. Went out there about four in the morning, took my time to it, stacked the bottles in one by one. Lucky there's a big hedge between that and the house next door. I was getting a kick out of it then," said Kindler, sounding wistful. "I kept getting more ideas, you know. I was just awful damn sorry I couldn't be around to see how Mrs. Burdick acted when she saw that skeleton sitting there."

"You'd probably have thought it worth the effort," said Maddox, wiping his eyes. "You do get ideas, friend."

"I suppose I shouldn't do any more?" said Kindler philosophically. "I'm sorry about that. You just can't imagine what a hell of a lot of fun it was. There was two I've been working on, going to do one tonight. This Mrs. Canning over on For-mosa, she nags her poor husband to death—he works at home, got a little tax-and-accounting business, so I'd heard her at him. Well, I know he's got a tape recorder, see, and what I was going to do, I was going to get one too—I got it yesterday —and sneak into the back yard some evening when they'd have the windows open, and tape a whole reel of her nag-nag-nag-ging at him. And then I'd do it up in fancy paper like a gift and send it to her by mail."

"Oh my God!" said Maddox. "What a diabolical—you do have ideas."

"What was the other one?" asked Rodriguez.

"Oh, that was a good one too. Old maid named Peters over on Detroit. She's got this little dog, see, one of those chihua-huas. Not a dog I'd like myself, but a nice enough little feller, and I tell you she's killing it with kindness. Feeds it candy all the time, and treats it like her own baby, you know what I mean. Doesn't know how to keep a dog proper, right feeding and all. Well, she goes out to a bridge club every Wednesday night—I used to bring her the postcards about it—and what I was going to do, the dog's out in the back yard when she's gone, was get in—dog knows me, see—and dress the dog all up in human baby clothes, to sort of point the moral, and then leave a copy of some good sensible book on how to treat dogs on the—"

They were all laughing. "Psychiatry for the man in the street." Rodriguez grinned. "Well, your little morality plays seem to have taken effect in two places at least, Mr. Kindler. But you really mustn't. I'm all with you in spirit, but tech-nically it is malicious mischief, you know."

"Well, it was a lot of fun," said Kindler. "You going to

make a charge on me, boys? Now you found out?"

"I don't think so," said Maddox. "Find out how the rest of them feel about it. Mrs. Endler was damn annoyed about the havoc that pig made of her garden."

"Oh, that so? I'm sorry. You tell her I'd be happy to pay any damages. And Mr. Rasmussen's doctor bills—I was sorry about that. But I guess, when they know it was me— Well, I guess all of 'em like me pretty well. I always tried to be friendly, you know— I don't suppose—"

"No," said Maddox, getting up. "I don't think we'll make an issue of it. But please, Mr. Kindler, curb your imagination. Find some other way of—of tinkering with human nature, will you? You've given us some laughs and maybe done a little good, but we really have enough work to do without—"

"I suppose," said Kindler regretfully. "But I did have some fun for a while there, boys."

"So back to Ruth and Ronnie," said Maddox. "Either of you brains have an idea on that?"

"Wedeck?" said D'Arcy. "We never really checked him out. That tax thing—kind of the irrational motive it could be."

"I don't see that," said Maddox. "I really don't. Oh hell, look anywhere and everywhere. Do you suppose we'd stand a chance of getting a search warrant for his home, the drug-store? If he's X, would he still have the gun?" He reminded himself that he wanted to call Morgan at the F.B.I., find out what they'd got questioning that Offenbach: hell, he could have had two guns of the same model. . . .

"All the ex-boy-friends," said Rodriguez.

Well, they could look. Go on looking.

They came into the lobby of the precinct and Carter said,

"Say, that's a cute little blonde, that Bergstrom girl, D'Arcy—one you were enlarging on to me yesterday. Quite a little dish. Only your timing's off, like César says." He grinned.

"She's *here*?" said D'Arcy excitedly. "She's—"

"Well, she was," said Carter. "She came in to ask if you'd found out anything yet, just an excuse, I sort of gathered. She seems to be interested in cops. Oh, a nice girl, I don't mean to say—"

"Sure she's a nice girl," said D'Arcy, glowering at him. "She's left? Damn the—"

"Well, that's what I say, your timing," said Carter. "If you'd been here—but you weren't, and Dick Brougham was. He'd just come in off something. He thought she was cute too. Last I saw, they went out together for a cup of coffee and he was asking if she had a date tonight."

"Oh, that bastard!" said D'Arcy. "That— Goddamn it, she ought to be warned about him—that Brougham, I'll—" He raged all the way up the stairs.

As they passed Ellis's office, Maddox stopped short. In there, perched on the chair beside the desk, sat Policewoman Carstairs. She was still in her finery, jade-green taffeta sheath, the green eye shadow, and the whole bit, and displaying rather a lot of sleek nylon-clad leg as she leaned back smoking reflectively—minus the cigarette holder.

"What the hell are you doing here?" asked Maddox.

"Oh, I got Ellis's precious evidence for him," said Policewoman Carstairs. "Finally. He's terribly pleased, ran off with the tape to get a warrant. Two warrants. Arrest and search." She ran a hand over her fashionable coiffure. "In fact, your little idea paid off, Maddox."

"Well, do tell. Gratifying. How?"

"About how we expected. I got a little note this morning,

with breakfast, asking would I kindly call at the manager's office at ten o'clock. So I did—having checked that damnable little device I was wearing tucked in my bra—and Mr. Cleveland was very fatherly. I started out all wide-eyed, was anything wrong, I'd kept my bill up to date and so on, and he patted my arm—he's rather like a toad," said Sue ruminatively, "something you find under a stone anyway—if you find toads there—and called me Little Lady. He said he'd been watching me and he saw what I was up to. Oh, it was all on a very high plane, no vulgar words spoken, you know, like that. And I was really stupid, trying it on my own. I could make much bigger money with far less trouble if I let him—er—manage me. He said I needn't worry, he knew the ropes, and I needn't go to all the trouble of finding the johns myself, just sit as a permanent guest in his hotel and wait for them to show up by appointment, connections all made by his agents. Or him. Of course I'd have to kick back a certain amount for all the services performed, as it were, but I'd find it a much better deal, really, and far safer. He said—" Sue looked amused— "you never knew when the vice cops were sniffing around, and sometimes they were hard to spot. I was being respectful and looking interested, and hoping to God that the device was working. I'd switched it on just before I went in."

"I take it, it did."

"Oh yes. Enough for the purpose. I was very grateful to kind Mr. Cleveland. I said it sounded like a fine deal and I'd certainly take him up on it, and I'd planned to do a little shopping this morning so if that was O.K. I'd see him later about the arrangements. And he patted my shoulder and told me I was a sensible girl and to run along now—so I ran right along back to base and handed Ellis the thing and we played it back. It's a little rough, but he came over quite plain. So

Ellis let out a sort of whoop and kissed me on both cheeks and dashed out after the warrants."

"Now *look*," said Maddox, "he's a respectable married man. And so now you can get out of the disguise, why the hell are you sitting around here looking like a poor man's Sadie Thompson?"

"I do not," said Policewoman Carstairs with dignity. "I look like a very fashionable and expensive Hollywood call girl. Mr. Cleveland said I had excellent taste in my dress. He also said I could expect to average about three grand a month. I'm thinking of resigning from the force and taking him up on it."

"For God's sake, go and wash your face," said Maddox. "And get back into uniform or at least a decent dress. You look like hell."

"There's gratitude for you," said Sue, putting out her cigarette and standing up. She smoothed green taffeta over one hip and batted her false eyelashes at Rodriguez. "Men are all alike, so I've heard tell. And cops no different. You do think up the messiest little jobs for us to do. And when it breaks in the *Times*, it'll be, Sergeant George Ellis made the arrest. I think I rather like the new hairdo, I'll keep it like this."

"You'll do no such thing," said Maddox. Ellis came up the stairs two at a stride, waving papers triumphantly.

"I've got the warrants—you hear about it? Just the way we hoped—hell of a break! You do have ideas, Ivor—you want to come and make the collar with me? By God, I said I'd get him."

"A break, he says," said Sue. "After I'd done all the work playing amateur dramatics all week."

"Yes, yes, you did a fine job, Sue, but what was so hard about it? You had—"

"I could take that as an insult, nothing difficult for me, play like a tart—but I won't," said Sue. "You just haven't any idea what a chore it is to put on false eyelashes and make them stick."

"Go wash your face," said Maddox. "All right, I'm with you, George."

The phone rang on Ellis's desk and he picked it up. "O.K.," he said after listening, "we're on it. . . . Daylight stickup at a bar over on Vine, bartender shot—D'Arcy, César, you get over there pronto—squad-car man got a description."

Always a little something turning up. On the whole, it had been a quiet week.

"What?" said Cleveland. "What? A *warrant?* This is ridiculous, gentlemen." He laughed heartily. He was, thought Maddox, rather like a toad—slab-faced, pasty complexion, bulging eyes, the would-be affable manner. Very nattily dressed, gold links, Sulka tie, and all.

"Some nice evidence, Cleveland," said Ellis happily. "Oh, such very nice evidence. A nice tape recording of the little interview you had awhile ago with the erstwhile Miss Sally Dupree, who's been staying here. You come over very clear, boy."

"What?" said Cleveland. "What do you— I don't—"

"Miss Dupree," said Maddox, "when she isn't doing a little amateur acting, is a policewoman stationed in this precinct, Mr. Cleveland. She's—um—quite the little amateur actress, isn't she?"

"What?" said Cleveland. He stared at them across the elegant slab-topped mahogany desk in his office. His mouth fell open stupidly.

"The—um—cleavage effect," said Maddox (feeling obscurely guilty about recalling that so clearly), "didn't extend to the miniature tape recorder. I understand it worked quite well."

"I am arresting you," began Ellis formally, "on a charge of—"

"That little brunette setup been operating out of my— A lady cop?" said Cleveland blankly. "A lady cop you're telling me. Jesus H. Christ, I don't believe—it ain't possible." He sat and stared at them.

"Quite a successful amateur actress," said Ellis pleasedly.

As per usual with Cleveland's type, they had no trouble with him. That kind very nonviolent. At intervals he kept muttering, "A lady cop—a lady cop. I don't believe it." He looked at them resentfully. "Jesus H. Christ, the bloodhounds start playing real dirty like that, a hell of a thing."

They booked him into the County Jail. They went to work, with Donaldson and O'Brien going through the Golden Cock Hotel. They turned up several females who were probably in Cleveland's string of call girls, and some interesting records in his desk drawers.

They got back to the precinct at four forty-five and asked D'Arcy about the stickup.

"The bartender was D.O.A.," said D'Arcy. "Three customers gave us some descriptions. César's downtown at Records with them going through mug shots. Nothing from Ballistics yet, but it looked like a heavy caliber."

So, something else to work. The routine. Heavy caliber—same as on Ruth and Ronnie.

And where the hell else to look on that? Maddox would like to get that one. Such a hell of an anonymous one.

Where?

Fifteen

Maddox called the F.B.I. office and asked for Morgan. "What've you got out of Offenbach?"

"Nothing. He's shut up like the proverbial clam. But I'm happy to say we got enough evidence to bring in Kramer and Kyser too. Don't tell me that gun checked out as the one you—"

"No, it didn't. But damn it, farfetched as it sounds, he could have had two of the same model. No, I know, if he just goes on saying no, I'd never prove different when I haven't got it. Why did they say they were collecting the arsenal, by the way?"

Morgan chuckled. "This little—ah—group Kramer was organizing—Citizens for Peace—all members were to be armed."

"Citizens for Peace?" said Maddox. "I see. Well, thanks."

"You've got nowhere, back to Offenbach again?"

"And the hell of it is, if he did it, I don't see I've got a chance in a million to prove it," said Maddox gloomily. "If he shows any signs of wanting to talk, let me know, will you?"

"Sure," said Morgan.

Maddox relayed that to D'Arcy. "If you say ex-boy-friends again—though I suppose we'll have to look. Where haven't we looked?"

"The amorous landlord Sandra told us about." D'Arcy scowled at the thought of his cute little blonde annexed by that wolf Brougham. "It could be."

"Almost anything could be," said Maddox.

"I've got to finish typing up this report on that stickup. I'll talk about Ruth and Ronnie with you later. I think we've gone about as far as we can on it." D'Arcy bent to the typewriter.

Maddox lit a cigarette and wondered. Ex-boy-friend, he thought. Ruth Evans a nice girl, a very pretty girl, a very serious girl; but by what they'd heard, she hadn't been the type to inspire such flaming passion that an ex-boy-friend would feel like killing her for taking up with someone else. And that probably said no to his little brainstorm that an anti-Semitic ex-boy-friend had got worked up about that: because he didn't think Ruth would have gone around with anybody who harbored any such feeling, and that would have been bound to come out.

All right. Where next? Cover the college again? César was no fool, he knew what he was doing and he was thorough; probably he'd got all there was to get there. And besides Maddox was still ninety percent sure X had been after Ruth, not Ronnie.

Then there was the gun. That was a small thought. If. Say X had already had it when he decided to go out on his shooting spree, then that was N.G., but if he'd had to go out and buy it— Better query all the pawnshops, the gunshops that had secondhand items for sale. Just for fun. You never knew, some simple little thing like that might lead them straight to him.

Rodriguez came in just as D'Arcy ripped the triplicate carbons from the typewriter. "Well, we may have cleaned this one up fast. You know we had three witnesses? One—"

"I haven't heard the details."

"Oh. Well, they hit that bar early, when there wouldn't be many customers. As a matter of fact they'd just opened, it was a damn-fool time to pull a holdup. Two customers, the owner and the bartender there. One of the customers an off-duty bank guard, retired from the Santa Monica force, so a trained observer. There were three of them, and one man stayed by the door, other two hit the bartender. The owner went for a forty-five he keeps by the cash register, and they exchanged a little fire. As D'Arcy probably told you, the bartender was D.O.A. Owner hit in the shoulder. But we got pretty good descriptions of two of 'em—the two gunmen—so I hustled the bank guard and the other customer downtown to look at mug shots, and they both spotted one man after we'd pored over about a thousand. He sounds good for it, and both identified him positively. Randolph Edgar Sims, aliases such and such, he's been in the pen twice for armed robbery, and he generally runs with two other fellows, his younger brother Jim and a pal named Alfred Mason—both of them have done time too, once on the same count as Sims."

"He sounds very nice," said Maddox.

"Yes. So I came home to pick up some help to bring them all in," said Rodriguez.

"Oh, do we know where they are?"

"We know where the two Simses are living, if they haven't moved, and they're both still on parole. Old hotel down on Rampart Boulevard. And just in case they are all three there gloating over their ill-gotten gold—oh, they rifled the register after the shooting, didn't get much. Well," said Rodriguez,

"Randolph Sims's official description says six-three, two hundred and ten, and his brother's nearly as big. I've got warrants."

"We'll all go," said Maddox. He looked at his watch. "If they're there, just nice time to fetch them back and turn them over to the night men for questioning."

They took two cars in case they picked up their quarry. The hotel on Rampart was an old shabby place, and its front looked somehow furtive, as if it was used to sheltering furtive men behind its façade. They went into the lobby and found a furtive-looking bald man sitting behind the counter.

"Have you a Randolph Sims still registered here?" asked Maddox. He'd be using his straight name because this was the address he'd given his parole officer. How very tired I am, thought Maddox suddenly, of these stupid louts who don't or can't think five minutes ahead. With his record, and on parole, he walks into that bar without even a stocking mask, and shoots a man dead for the day's starting money in the till. Well, this time, it was to be hoped, he'd be put away for good and all, on a homicide. Though you never knew. If he got life instead of the gas chamber, in this state he'd be eligible for parole in just seven years, and really, how unrealistic could the ivory-tower legislators get? It did make you wonder. He watched the bald man slowly searching the register, and his mind went back to Ruth and Ronnie. The tough one. The one he'd like to get.

"Room three-oh-nine," said the bald man reluctantly. He looked at them with dislike: all three of them quite ordinary-looking young men, except for D'Arcy's beanpole height, and the average citizen wouldn't have turned to look at them in the street, but the bald man smelled the law at once, didn't need a second look. "There's not gonna be any trouble, is there?" he asked nervously.

"That's up to Mr. Sims," said D'Arcy. "Would you know if he's in?"

The bald man glanced at the rack behind him. "He's got his key, anyways."

"So," said Maddox. They turned to the one very ancient self-service elevator and rode up to the third floor in silence.

"Sims the elder," said Rodriguez as they emerged into a bare corridor smelling of dust and unwashed bodies, "has a record for hitting first and asking who afterward."

"Thanks so much for the warning," said Maddox. They tried to move quietly on the bare wooden floor. They came to 309 and paused, and in mutual silent agreement all drew their .38's. It was rather rarely you had to use the gun, though it was regulation to carry it, but on some occasions it was convenient and comforting to have it there, and if the witnesses were right Sims had shot a man this morning.

Maddox knocked on the door lightly.

Beyond the door a chair scraped back on bare floor and a man's voice said, "That's Al with the booze. Jesus, I can use a—" The door opened.

"Boo," said Maddox. "Don't do any reaching, friend. We want you."

"Jim!" yelled the big man in the doorway, and dodged back into the room. A gun went off very close. Maddox fired a snap shot at the second man in the room, missed him, and then D'Arcy was on him, got him down, and wrested the gun away. Rodriguez was busy wrestling with the other man; as Maddox turned Sims got the smaller Rodriguez on the jaw and knocked him down. He plunged for the bureau—probably after a gun—

and Maddox snapped, "Hold it, Sims! Hold it right there or you get it in the back!"

Sims held it. Rodriguez got up feeling his jaw and brushing himself down fastidiously; D'Arcy hauled the other man up. They put the cuffs on them, ignoring all the cussing, and Maddox said, "You know, I think it might be profitable to hang around a few minutes. Evidently Al went out to buy a couple of bottles, and if he didn't hear those shots—" Nobody in a place like this would be apt to come running to ask about those shots.

"In that case, hadn't we better gag this pair before they—"

"Hey, lemme in," said a plaintive voice in the hall. "I got my hands full." D'Arcy clapped an arm across Randolph Sims's mouth and Rodriguez obliged for the other one. Maddox swung the door open.

"Come right in, Mr. Mason. But I'm afraid we can't let you take the bottles with you to jail. Very moral fellows, those bailiffs."

"Hey!" said Mason, staring. "Hey! How'd you—" He was taken entirely by surprise.

"Oh, you damn stupid louts," said Maddox tiredly. "With your mug shots for anybody to look at down in Records, you pull a job and trot right back to the address you gave the P.A. officer, and you're surprised as hell when we drop on you." But of course this kind of dumb pro always did that sort of thing: they posed a problem, but not any mysteries.

Well, on a homicide charge they'd probably all share, with any luck and a judge with any sense, they'd get more than a seven-to-ten this time. Third count for the elder Sims, too.

They took them down to the County Jail and booked them in. It was after six by that time so they drove back to the

Grotto for drinks and dinner. "I want," said Maddox, "to talk to the Evanses again. Forlorn hope maybe but maybe too they've thought of something. I'd appreciate any little new scrap of something. I never knew such a damn case. Every single lead we get fizzling out to nothing." He contemplated his drink gloomily.

The waitress for their table, like Miss Sandra Bergstrom, liked cops; she liked the Wilcox Street men coming in, it was interesting. She figured tonight, by Sergeant Maddox's expression, they were having bad luck at whatever job they were working, and she was sorry. If Jim had been busy at the bar and she'd had their drinks to make, she'd have slipped in a little extra. As it was, she personally picked out their steaks and gave them to the chef with strict orders. Sergeant Maddox always looked a bit underweight, she thought; and that Detective Rodriguez was handsome, all right, but there was just something *about* Sergeant Maddox—

"There is also," said Maddox, starting on his steak without noticing its quality much, "the amorous landlord."

"I might consider him," said Rodriguez, "if you'll tell me how he knew Ruth's name, how he found out where she lived, and even if he is a little or a lot lunatic, why he wanted to kill her for resisting his advances."

"Well, it still looks like an irrational motive. He could be a nut, César. From what D'Arcy's new flame told us, in fact, he must be—grabbing a casual visitor like that and trying to drag her into his apartment. In fact, if that was so—we don't know that Ruth didn't exaggerate it some. I'd be surprised if there haven't been other complaints on him. And if Ruth was as dedicated to her job as everyone says, she should have known a guy like that should have been reported."

"But why should she exaggerate it?" asked D'Arcy.

"Who knows? Anyway, come to think if she told Sandra she may have mentioned it to her parents. Did you get the landlord's address, César?"

"Got it somewhere. Let's have dinner in peace, shall we?" Rodriguez pulled out a paperback copy of *Lady Killer* and looked at it wistfully. "This McBain is very damn good, isn't he?"

"Very. At least," said Maddox, "you're keeping out of any extracurricular trouble since you got involved with all the detective novels. . . ."

They got to Franklin Avenue at eight o'clock. The house was nearly dark, and they wondered if the Evanses were there; but Evans opened the door.

"Oh—" he said. "Something—something more, gentlemen? Have you—"

"Not yet, Mr. Evans, I'm sorry. This is being a very tough one," said Maddox. "Mind if we ask a few more questions?"

"No, of course not. Come in, won't you? I'm sorry, my wife had a headache and went to bed early." He was the neat, well-spoken, good-looking professional man, but a second glance showed the haggard expression, the tired lines about the eyes. "I don't know what else I could tell you—I—there was just no reason— Please sit down."

"Do you remember Ruth ever mentioning the landlord at a place where one of her cases lived?"

"A *landlord*. No, I don't, I'm sorry. Was it—somebody like that— Something in her job? Oh God, I can't understand—"

"We don't know, Mr. Evans. We're just snatching at every small lead we get." Maddox started to take him through it all again: first, his every minute recollection of what he'd seen and heard that night. A week ago tonight, when Ruth and Ronnie had had a date, the two nice responsible young people —and come home to keep a date with death. And then about Ruth: friends, boy friends, any arguments she'd had with anyone, any difficulties she had mentioned. And there was nothing. She had liked her job, taken it seriously, believed in the work she was doing. The Evanses had liked Ronnie, approved of the engagement. Nobody in the family had any remote bit of prejudice against Jews or anybody else; that couldn't have been a factor, said Evans a little angrily. He knew there wasn't anybody who could have had any reason to want to kill Ruth, so whatever incomprehensible motive there could have been, it must have been on Ronnie. But that was nearly as fantastic.

"He was such a—a good fellow." Evans stared at his clasped hands. "Oh, I don't mean goody-goody. Like that. But a lot more serious than a lot of fellows his age, and you knew he'd get places." On that, he smiled bitterly. "Would have . . . A very conservative young chap, even though he was young. I remember that night—when he came to call for Ruth—she wasn't quite ready and we sat here talking a few minutes." He passed a hand across his face: that last time when things had been normal, as-expected: the time before nightmare. "He was asking me if I'd ever heard of this organization, he'd just heard about it and he thought it might be a Communist-front thing, he'd thought of asking the F.B.I., passing on what he—"

A sudden wild thought hit Maddox. "Would it have been a group called Citizens for Peace?"

"What? Oh no, I forget what he said it was—some one of the other students at the college had tried to get him interested in it. He did say he'd talked it all over with his uncle, the previous weekend, so Goldfarb could probably tell you more about— The New Pacifists, that was it, just came to me. For God's sake, Sergeant, you can't think— It's ridiculous. There's just *nothing*, no reason. Two good, productive young lives snuffed out, for *nothing*."

"It doesn't seem to make much sense, Mr. Evans," agreed Maddox. Did that say anything at all? On one as vague as this, anything could point the way. The New Pacifists. Citizens for Peace. The new double-talk, thought Maddox. But people like that really didn't go roaring around with .45's murdering the unbelievers. Well, did they? There was Offenbach with his arsenal.

He asked more questions. No, Ruth had never— Well, said Evans, he did remember, when she'd been in college, that one fellow had tried to date her several times, a Southern chap he'd been, but she didn't like him because he was, she said, terribly prejudiced. She'd never gone out with him for that reason, and really, five years ago—and no, Evans didn't recall his name.

Nothing, nothing, nothing. Neither Ruth nor Ronnie had been angels; there had undoubtedly been some people who hadn't liked them for this reason or that, or been indifferent to them; but as young people went these days (God, twenty-five and twenty-seven) they had been young people of great integrity, serious and ambitious. Most of their friends would have been the same kind. Nobody had disapproved of their intended marriage. The only jealousy that showed up was on the Ferguson girl, and a hundred percent sure she was out of it. Oh, check and see: look at that apartment, but—

And it was still open on Offenbach. That one. You did indeed sometimes wonder how far the human animal had made progress. . . . And if it had been Offenbach, a million to one they'd never prove it, when he'd got rid of the gun.

Maddox thought about Offenbach. A little wistfully he thought about him: because he knew the Offenbachs were ninety-nine hundredths all bluster and bluff and bad temper —little, fearful, cowardly men in their souls: and if you got one of them where you could use your fists and maybe a sap or a few lighted matches, he'd come apart at the seams as of now. Most unfortunately, there were a lot of rules and regulations about that sort of thing, these days, and an upright L.A.P.D. man shouldn't even let the thought cross his mind.

He sighed. If it had been Offenbach, they'd never know.

Maybe they'd never know anyway.

"Well, thanks, Mr. Evans," he said.

"It isn't that I'm *vindictive*," said Evans to him at the door. "I don't think." He gave Maddox a painful smile. "But you've got to get whoever—whoever—whatever madman— Because anyone who could do *that*—would kill again. Anyone. You've got to—"

"We'd like to very much," said Maddox. "It's a tough one. But we'll keep on looking, Mr. Evans."

Until, he thought, the pressure of other cases and the hopelessness of finding anything new on this forced them to file it away under Pending. Sometimes one like that came along. But it wasn't generally the offbeat thing like this one; it was usually just the anonymous crime, assault to robbery to rape to homicide, where there just wasn't enough evidence to follow.

Ruth and Ronnie rather definitely the offbeat thing.

Maddox woke before the alarm went off on Saturday morning, and lay for a while thinking. Sheila's party tonight. Probably need the alarm tomorrow morning. Damn women. Well, both interesting and necessary, but—

The New Pacifists. Ronnie going to the F.B.I. and— That was ridiculous. Grasping at straws. People like that—

His trained detective's mind said, People like what? You don't know anything about the New Pacifists. Could be a blind for an espionage ring. These days— And could be they weren't in a position to stand any investigation, and if Ronnie had alerted the F.B.I.—

Ridiculous. A crackpot college-students group, and Ronnie quite openly solicited to it by another college student. Somebody, obviously, who wasn't aware of Ronnie's politics. That said nothing.

Offenbach. Mentally he consigned Offenbach to the nethermost depths of hell (if they only knew about the bastard one way or the other!), got up, shaved, dressed, made coffee, and got to Wilcox Street at ten to eight.

Rodriguez had given him the address: Grand Avenue, downtown. At eight forty he and D'Arcy got there, found a slot for the Frazer-Nash. It was the oldest part of L.A. here, very shabby and run down, the street dirty, the buildings ancient tumbledown frames. The apartment house where the Reyes family lived—one of Ruth's cases—was four-story, more recently painted than its immediate neighbors.

"This is really reaching," said D'Arcy sourly.

"So on this one maybe we've got to," said Maddox. They went in. There was a long narrow dark corridor: a door marked with a hand-lettered sign, SUPERINTENDENT. Maddox rang the bell. A woman opened the door instantly and looked at them.

She was sloppily dressed, dark, buxom, brown-eyed, about forty.

"Yes?"

"We'd like to see Mr. Zecchino," said Maddox.

"He's not here," said the woman dully. She looked at them again. Down here also, the citizenry could smell the law. "You're cops," she said. "You oughta know he isn't here, he's in jail. They finally come and got him. Yesterday. And past time, way he carried on. I'm his sister, I could tell them. Just lucky he hadn't raped nobody yet. I don't figure he's exactly right in the head since Rita up and left him. His wife."

"Oh really," said Maddox. "What was the charge?"

"I don't know, I wasn't here when they come. Some woman complained, I suppose. Serve him right, way he's been acting. I'm not going bail for him, I can tell you that. And now I'm in charge here, if his name is still on the deed, I don't 'specially want the fuzz in my place," she said expressionlessly, and stepped back and slammed the door.

"Well, well," said Maddox. "Are we chasing a wild goose or aren't we? I think we now contact the big brains at Central and find out what Zecchino got picked up for."

"I think so too," said D'Arcy.

They went up to the big Police Facilities Building and asked questions. They were, probably, chasing a wild goose. There had been a number of complaints on Zecchino over the last eighteen months; he had accosted several women who lived in the apartment house, making lewd remarks, snatching kisses, attempting to coerce them into his apartment. None of them had wanted to press charges, and there hadn't been anything to take him in for, up to yesterday. Yesterday, a young woman had hailed the squad car on the beat and complained that Zecchino had tried to assault her in the hallway of the apartment. She exhibited bruises, she was in a towering rage, her name was Margarita Teresa Rosetta Confarsi, and she was more than willing to sign a formal complaint. So Central had picked up Zecchino, and he was in the new jail facility on Alameda awaiting arraignment.

Maddox and D'Arcy went to see him and asked him questions. They got nothing. It emerged pretty clearly that he hadn't known Ruth Evans's name; just that she was the social worker who came visiting the Reyes family, and a pretty girl.

He was under psychiatric examination.

"So what?" asked D'Arcy. "Ask for a search warrant and go over his apartment for the gun?"

"Oh my God," said Maddox, "talk about reaching! He's way off the beam, I don't need a head doctor to tell me, but he didn't even know her name, for God's sake. . . . I tell you, D'Arcy, it's a real bastard. We'll never get X. Because there wasn't any motive that looks like a motive, damn it. Damn it. The New Pacifists. . . ."

"You are really letting your Celtic imagination run wild there," said D'Arcy.

"Buy you a cup of coffee," said Maddox. It was a little past ten thirty and they were back in Hollywood; he turned on Santa Monica and parked in the Grotto's lot. They went in; Rodriguez was sitting with Sue Carstairs talking animatedly over a cup of coffee, and Maddox and D'Arcy joined them.

"Another dead end," said Rodriguez, eyeing Maddox.

"What it comes to," said Maddox angrily, "is we'll file it away. Damn it. I never *knew* such a case. Every damn lead we get—" He sat down. "So all right, tell me I'm crazy," he said abruptly. "The New Pacifists. Yes. You know something? I think it was Offenbach, and damn it to hell, we'll never get him for it. But if it wasn't—if it wasn't—"

"The New Pacifists?" said Sue. "Don't fuss, Ivor. You'll get there in the end. Maddox the brain."

"All *right*, I'm crazy," said Maddox. "They're going to dynamite the City Hall and Ronnie was going to report them to the Feds and they couldn't stand any investigation."

"The New *Pacifists*?" said Rodriguez.

"And Ronnie had talked it all over with his uncle," said Maddox. "I think I want to see Goldfarb again."

"Reaching you can say," said D'Arcy. "Goldfarb never mentioning it, never thinking about it, if it was the spy-thriller thing and Ronnie'd told him all about it? And how'd Ronnie find out? A silly college-boys' club, I ask you!"

"So I'm reaching," said Maddox. "I want to ask Goldfarb." He got up.

Sixteen

THERE WAS A PUBLIC PHONE IN THE LOBBY; HE USED IT TO CALL the Goldfarb home out in Duarte. When he got back to the table the coffee had arrived. "Goldfarb's over at Ronnie's apartment, still clearing things up. At least we don't have to drive out to Duarte."

"I don't know why you want to see him at all," said D'Arcy. "The New Pacifists, yet."

"On a thing like this, you look at everything," said Maddox. The coffee was nearly too hot to drink; the waitress who liked cops had firm opinions about coffee, if it was hot it ought to be *hot*. He added a little cream to it.

"César's been telling me about Mr. Kindler," said Sue. "I could easily fall in love with Mr. Kindler. I do like a man to have a sense of humor."

Maddox grinned. "He's got that all right."

"I'd love," said Sue, "to have seen that pig."

"Oh my God, that pig. The funny thing is, he seems to have accomplished something. Evidently Endler's eased off on the drinking, and Rasmussen's promised to reform too."

"You don't," said Rodriguez, "seriously believe that these Pacifists had one damn thing to do with Ruth and Ronnie, do you? Because I've heard you using your wild imagination before, but that is about the wildest I've known you to get."

"I don't know," said Maddox, sounding goaded. "I just know somebody had that S. and W. army revolver, somebody killed them, for some damn reason, and there's got to be a lead to find somewhere. You'd think, a week on it, we'd have got something. I'm just taking a look at everything that shows, the hell with how farfetched it looks." He drank coffee moodily.

"Well, I see that. I just say the Pacifists are a little bit too farfetched," said Rodriguez.

They sat in silence awhile, drinking coffee. Sue said without much conviction she ought to be getting back, and continued to sit. "After this last exotic week, it seems terribly tame dealing with the juveniles and typing up reports." She was looking like Policewoman Carstairs again, in a neat navy dress, her crisp dark hair in a plain tailored wave.

"At least you look respectable again," said Maddox. "Never saw a man get such a shock as Cleveland—he couldn't believe it. Seemed to feel we'd been playing dirty pool, taking advantage of him like that."

They relapsed into silence again. "But who could have done it?" said Sue suddenly. "That young couple. It doesn't make sense—nobody would have had any reason."

"I know, I know," said Maddox. "We've been on the merry-go-round all week, one little lead after another. No rhyme nor reason to it. But they're dead, Sue. Dead and buried. I'd like to know why, and I'd like to know who, but I'm beginning to think we never will."

"—Deliberately waited for them up there at the Evanses' house, to shoot them. You haven't turned up anything?"

"Nothing at all remotely useful. So I'm grasping at straws. You can see why." Maddox finished his coffee, put out his cigarette, and stood up. "Come on, D'Arcy, let's go find those straws."

"Wild blue yonder," said D'Arcy, unfolding his lank frame.

"Well, good luck on it," said Sue.

"Thanks. See you." Maddox lifted a casual hand; he and D'Arcy went out.

Rodriguez cocked one brow at Policewoman Carstairs. "You'll never get him, Sue," he said. "I don't think he's the marrying kind of man."

Policewoman Carstairs said coldly, "For heaven's sake, César! Who would want him? A—a husband every female under forty in L.A. County was chasing like mad?"

"I rather think," said Rodriguez thoughtfully, "that's why he's avoided it up to now—cautious fellow, our little Welshman. Figures it wouldn't be fair to a legal wife."

"In which he is quite right," said Sue. "And in any case, any woman who gets involved with a cop is out of her mind. Absolutely. I've got to get back. See you."

"Mmh," said Rodriguez. He watched her out. A nice girl, Carstairs. If Maddox ever did get down to one permanent, he could do worse.

He ought to be getting back too, thought Rodriguez. Something new might have come up. He pulled a paperback copy of *The Pusher* out of his pocket. This fellow was very damn good. Oh well, ¿pues y qué?—take another ten minutes.

He beckoned the waitress and ordered more coffee, sat back and opened his book.

When Maddox and D'Arcy got to Mrs. Barker's house on

Ardmore Avenue, they found Goldfarb at the open trunk of a year-old Olds parked in front of the house, putting a carton inside. He straightened as they came up.

"Have you found out anything, Sergeant?"

"It's a very tough one," said Maddox. "A few more questions if you don't mind, Mr. Goldfarb."

"I don't mind, anything at all I can do to help you." Goldfarb hopped up on the curb. "I've been—clearing up. Mrs. Barker wants to have the place free to rent, of course. Sorting out all his things. I think maybe that's the worst about somebody dying, Sergeant. All the things they leave behind, all of a sudden so damn unimportant. Maybe things they valued, you know—it just sort of came to me just now when I came across that expensive tie he liked. He splurged to buy it, see, said it was silly at the time, but he liked it. French import, it was. I'd forgot about it till just now. Maybe we ought to have buried him in it." His voice shook a little. "And what was it when I picked it up out of the drawer there? Just an old tie. To go in with the things for salvage." He was silent, and then he said, "I often think that's the worst of it, having to go through the things. There's not much, but of course it's got to be sorted out."

"Yes sir," said Maddox.

"Somebody's got to do it. His clothes can go to the salvage people. There's a pair of gold links belonged to Joe—his dad—I'll keep those. And his mother's engagement ring."

They were walking around Mrs. Barker's front house, slowly, by the little cement path.

"And then it's finished," said Goldfarb. "It's done. It's like he'd never been. A good boy—and all he'd done, all his plans, the way he had to go through all that after the accident, the bone grafts and all. Why, Sergeant? What's it all for, what does it mean?"

"I only wish I knew, Mr. Goldfarb."

"I'd just," said Goldfarb, "like to know why. I guess I never was very religious, we were Reform but not much given to—you know—keeping up with temple. You say the words, anybody asks you, you say, yes, you believe in God. But do I? Do I? A senseless thing like this happens, there's a God planning out everything for the best? I don't believe that. I can't believe that, Sergeant."

"We don't know all the answers," said Maddox. "I know, Mr. Goldfarb."

"Because there's something like God—something—something rational, you know, making plans—holding all the strings —they'd be, well, rational plans, wouldn't they? Like cause and effect. Like that. And here's two people, hardly begun to live yet, all full of all sorts of plans, and they've worked hard and—you know—like sacrificed things, to get where they were. And all the medical bills for Ronnie, and how game he was, going through all that because he had all these plans for the future. And Ruth, now, all she'd done and planned and the Evanses so proud of her—same as we were of Ronnie—and all of a sudden, bang, it's all wiped out, they're just nothing and all that gone. For nothing. Nothing. That doesn't make any sense to me, Sergeant."

"It doesn't make much to me," said Maddox. He thought a moment and then he said, " 'The day of death is when two worlds meet with a kiss: this world going out, the future world coming in.' "

"You know the Talmud, Sergeant? Yes, a lot of fine words

about it. I don't know. I just don't know. Do you believe that, Sergeant?"

"I don't know either." Maddox could remember the Sunday-school teacher in that long-ago class, the Sunday feel of his best clothes and the nice little stories about the saints, and memorizing the psalms for prizes. He hadn't gone much after his mother died. *Yea, though I walk through the valley of the shadow of death, I will fear no evil—*

Fear no evil, he thought. He had always rather admired the sagacity and downright honesty of that tribe somewhere in East Africa—couldn't remember which—who, frankly declaring that God or any such thing was completely unknowable by man, uttered their prayers to the Dark and the Unknown. A very sensible procedure.

"Well, come in," said Goldfarb. "Come in."

In the little three-room house Mrs. Barker was alternately cleaning and crying. Goldfarb had evidently nearly finished sorting out Ronnie's possessions; another cardboard carton of clothes rested near the front door, and the desk had been swept clean. Mrs. Barker was washing the front windows.

"It won't seem natural, having somebody else here," she said mournfully. "Instead of Ronnie. That little maple table was his, Mr. Goldfarb. I just furnished the place with odds and ends, and he picked it up secondhand."

"I guess you'd better keep it," said Goldfarb. He sat down on the little couch, D'Arcy sat beside him, and Maddox took the one armchair. "You haven't found out anything, Sergeant? That fellow you mentioned, the Nazi—"

"Well, he could have, but there's really nothing that says so for sure. I don't think he did." Because, come to think,

Offenbach and Kramer and Kyser had been getting their kicks —and keeping fairly busy—with the little hate group and all the printed pamphlets, hadn't they? "Did Ronnie ever mention an organization called the New Pacifists to you?"

Goldfarb looked up in surprise. "Why, yes, he did. Just a couple of weeks ago. For God's sake, Sergeant, you don't think it was—was that kind of motive, do you? A thing like—that doesn't make sense either."

"Well, just tell me what you recall about it."

"Sure, but— Well, another fellow at the college had been trying to get new members for it. Buttonholing students in the cafeteria and handing out pamphlets and so on. He gave one to Ronnie, and Ronnie didn't like the smell of it. Neither did I when he showed it to me. It was—" Goldfarb rubbed his nose absently—"full of double-talk about how both parties are secret military parties and all the time plotting war to keep the economy up, and all patriotic Americans who want real peace must rise and demand an end to all the missile building and— You know, kind of thing to appeal to young people with idealistic notions, and could be it's just a bunch of youngsters like that, but also could be it's a Commie thing. Front." Goldfarb smiled faintly. "Ideals, they're just fine," he said. "But in this life, you got to deal with facts—and with human nature. I always liked that one—forget who said it, would it be Benjamin Franklin?—that any man who isn't a Socialist by the time he's twenty-five hasn't got a heart, and any man who isn't a Tory by the time he's thirty hasn't got a head."

Maddox grinned. "Disraeli, I think, wasn't it?"

"Mr. Goldfarb," said D'Arcy, "did Ronnie—was he enough worried by this that he was considering taking it to the F.B.I.?"

"Why, I don't think so. We talked it all over, and I asked

him if this fellow was trying to annex members all openly, and seemed he was, and there was notice of a meeting at somebody's house, nothing secret about it, and I told him I figured if it was a Commie thing the G-men probably knew all about it anyway, sharp as they are. I don't get this—that couldn't have anything to do—"

"We're just looking everywhere," said Maddox.

"Did you get his transistor radio?" asked Mrs. Barker suddenly. "Oh dear, I haven't really taken it in yet—so sudden. It just doesn't seem *possible*. All the plans and ambitions he had." She bent and picked up a folded newspaper from the straight chair, automatically thrust it into the wastebasket by the desk. "What are you going to do with all his books?"

"I guess," said Goldfarb, "I'll tell the college, maybe, give them to anybody needs them. Fellow trying to get a legal education, those books can run into money." He looked at Maddox: "We've got nobody now, you see. Never had any ourselves, and I guess—we sort of had all our eggs in one basket, with Ronnie."

"There was a young fellow he knew," said Maddox, "the one who came and told us about Offenbach. Ed Williams. Young Negro. Seems like a nice young man—legal student too, I don't know how far along, he looks about twenty-two. Father's a truck driver."

"He'd be a good one to give them to," said Goldfarb heavily.

Maddox's mind was now a complete blank. He just didn't see where else to go, where to ask questions, what questions to ask, on Ruth and Ronnie.

All they knew, seven days later, was just exactly what they'd known at two A.M. last Saturday morning, when Joe Rowan had responded to the squad car's call for a detective. They

211 —

knew that Ruth and Ronnie had come home after a date, and were parked in the driveway of the Franklin Avenue house—talking or necking—and they knew that somebody had been waiting for them to come home, in that yard next door beyond the hedge. Somebody who had, maybe, done some trampling around in the flower bed there, maybe had smoked a couple of cigarettes, waiting. And when they showed up, the somebody had opened fire, and stopped to reload after emptying the gun once, and emptied it again. And killed them both.

The only single solitary fact they knew now which Rowan hadn't known at two A.M. last Saturday morning was what gun had been used. A Smith and Wesson 1950 army model revolver.

That was nice going for a week on the case, wasn't it? He thought about Sheila's party tonight. Maybe cheer him up a bit. Sheila . . .

Mrs. Barker had finished the windows and now took up the smallish cotton throw rug in the living room. "Practical," she said. "Goes right in the washer. And that was another thing, he was so good about keeping things neat 'n' clean. Most young men—but he always liked things tidy. You don't have any *idea* who did it? After a week? Must have been a lunatic, all I can think—"

But he had waited for Ruth and Ronnie. He knew who he wanted. Not altogether a lunatic.

"Sergeant."

"Yes, Mr. Goldfarb."

"I suppose it could have been—just a nut with a gun. And we'll never know."

"I don't think so," said Maddox.

"Because he waited up there for them, sir," said D'Arcy.

"Deliberately. A lunatic wouldn't care who he shot."

"Oh," said Goldfarb. "Yes, I see that. But—" he fell silent. He said, "It'd be good to be able to believe in a God like that, planning. Have some kind of faith that—that there was a bigger plan we just don't know about yet."

"Yes," said Maddox. "It would. Maybe there is."

Mrs. Barker came back from the kitchen. "I'd cleaned out the refrigerator last week, of course. After—after I heard. It's just to get things straight for anybody coming in. The bedding's all mine except for that yellow plaid blanket, did you get that, Mr. Goldfarb?"

"What? No, I didn't know—you'd better keep it, I guess."

"Well, thank you, it's a nice blanket." She began to sweep the floor vigorously. "You got to keep after these old pine floors, not like hardwood, they do attract the dirt." She swept briskly in the area by the door, working toward them.

"Seems some—you know—clue should have showed up," said Goldfarb.

"Something usually does in this time," said Maddox.

"I'll have to ask you to move in a minute," said Mrs. Barker. "I'm sorry." She wielded the broom, and a small object skittered across the bare floor and hit Maddox's left shoe. He bent and picked it up.

"Oh, excuse me," said Mrs. Barker. She came and took it from him. "One of those disposable filters from his cigarette holder. He's always used one since he read that report—and sometimes he'd come to see Ronnie here—"

A small cold finger trailed up Maddox's spine. "Who, Mrs. Barker?"

"Oh, Mr. Rhys. Poor old fellow." She dropped the used filter into the wastebasket.

Maddox stood up and D'Arcy stood with him. They looked at each other. "Mrs. Barker, where exactly does Mr. Rhys live?" asked Maddox very gently.

"Why, three houses down— Mrs. Waterman's got a little house on the back of her lot too, he rents that. Why—"

"Does he drive a car?"

"Yes, he's got an old Pontiac he drives sometimes, not much. He rents her garage too. It gives her a little something extra, you see, she's a widow like me, only of course she's a lot older and terrible deaf, you can hardly—"

"I see," said Maddox. He moved to the door with D'Arcy after him. "Thanks, Mr. Goldfarb."

Goldfarb had risen too. "Sergeant—you're not telling me— you're not thinking—" He had heard the finality, the cold conclusion, in Maddox's voice; his eyes held awful incredulity. "You don't—"

"Come on, D'Arcy," said Maddox.

They found him waiting for them, sitting in an old padded armchair in the little living room of the house behind the deaf Mrs. Waterman's house. This little house a lot less tidy than Ronnie's had been: old furniture, and the windows needed washing, and it smelled a little of old man, of elderly life lived frugally.

He sat in the armchair, and he was holding the gun in his lap. When they knocked at the door he didn't get up, just told them to come in. The gun was the first thing they saw.

"Mr. Rhys—" said Maddox.

"I thought I'd have the guts to do it," said the old man. "I did—to kill myself. But I haven't. I don't want to die. I know I'm maybe most nearly dead but I don't want to. But you've found out, haven't you? Found—out—it—was—me."

"Yes," said Maddox. He bent and picked up the gun from the old man's limp fingers. It was a Smith and Wesson 1950 army model revolver. This time it would be the right one. Ballistics would tell them.

"I did it. I shot him. I *killed* him. Oh dear Jesus, I never meant to do that. I never meant—I never— I just wanted him back!" Suddenly Rhys began to cry quietly. "Don't know what it means to an old man— Somebody friendly, nice, to talk to—somebody *interested* in you—listen to you, not just being sorry but *liking* you—like that. You don't know, you don't know! Come to play checkers with me and talk—and bring magazines, kind, he was good, I knew he was studying and all but he took the time come and be kind to me. I got nobody else. Nobody. It gets lonely for an old man alone, nobody his own to take a little interest. And then he come and he told me—going to get married, and he showed me her picture and he told me all about her—how pretty and nice she was and all. And I thought, that was good."

"Yes, Mr. Rhys?"

"But—but it changed. You got to understand why. Oh Christ, I been in hell ever since—ever since. I guess I deserve go to hell, I was tryin' to get up the guts—shoot myself, or come tell you just how it was. It all changed. Everything. He didn't come near so often any more. He'd be with *her*. That girl. He didn't take the time come and play checkers with me, talk to me, listen to me. You don't *know* how much it means to an old man. Nights he'd come, Sunday afternoons sometimes, it was like—like when you're a kid and there's a special treat. You got to understand it. He didn't come, then, after that. Or just to bring me the books, the magazines, say, got a date with Ruth, and off he'd go. You don't know how I *missed* him. Nobody else, last few years. Nobody. It gets lonely. It gets lonely.

"And I'd think of her. Taking him away. Young people don't know—don't stop to think." Rhys had stopped crying; he mopped at his eyes. "Young people— She didn't know, but she took him away from me. I haven't much time left, and I wanted it like it was before, him coming and everything nice and comfortable, and the checkers and the talking. It wouldn't be long, I'm an old man. I'd think about her and how she'd taken him away. I never meant—*him*. Oh my dear God. Not Ronnie. Not Ronnie. But—but—but I thought, if she wasn't *there*—he couldn't marry her. It was bad enough—her taking him away—so he didn't come so often—but he came sometimes, only after they were married he'd be moving away—with *her*—and never come no more. Never. You got to see. He was young, he had lots of time, he could find another girl. But me, I haven't got time. All I wanted was—like it was before. The other times, he'd come the whole evening, talk, play checkers. Like that. All I wanted.

"I'd think about her. He told me all about her. I never met her, you know. I didn't think about her like a—like a—live person, you got to— Just a thing took him away so he wasn't interested, didn't come by no more. And I thought—I thought if she wasn't *there*—it'd all get like it used to be—with Ronnie.

"I had the gun. Had it a long time. It belonged to Mrs. Waterman's husband, she give it to me, she liked have somebody on the premises could hear a burglar, you know. And I thought—I knew where that girl lived. He said, family got money. I don't drive much any more but I went up there one day and looked. And I thought—I thought it'd be easy to—Wait till he brought her home, and—

"So that's what I did. Only I never meant—never *meant*—him too! I—I—I—didn't think—maybe he'd be kissing her good night—and it was dark, I had to make sure—and so I reloaded the gun. *I never meant Ronnie.*"

"We understand, Mr. Rhys," said Maddox. Mrs. Barker had said, One stroke already. Little brain damage? Probably. Hadn't he meant Ronnie, unconsciously? For going away from him—to youth. As he'd see it intuitively. Ronnie, good and kind, sorry for the old man—but Ronnie young, with life ahead.

Only there had been only death.

"I just wanted it like it was. She'd took him away, he didn't have time for me no more," said Rhys. "And it gets lonely for an old man."

"Mr. Rhys," said Maddox. He handed the gun to D'Arcy and put a hand under Rhys's elbow. "You know we'd like you to come with us now."

The old man looked up at him. "Yes sir," he said in a docile tone. "I tried make myself come tell you. *Ronnie.* I never meant— I only wanted things back like they used to be. And she took him away. But I killed Ronnie too and I never meant—"

Maddox got him up on his feet, led him out. D'Arcy was wearing an incredulous expression; he said, "Offbeat, let us say. Any fag undertones?"

"Not a smell," said Maddox evenly. "It was just what he tells us it was."

Rhys came beside him meekly, silent now, his head bent

and shoulders hunched. The Frazer-Nash was parked up in front of the Barker house; and as they approached it Maddox saw Goldfarb standing there, motionless at the curb beside the Olds, keys dangling from one hand, staring at them.

And Robert Rhys saw him too, and as they came up he looked at Ronnie's uncle and he fell to his knees on the sidewalk and he cried incoherently, "I never meant—I'm sorry, I'm sorry, in hell I've been— Ronnie too— I only wanted— things back like they were before she took him away—coming and being kind—only wanted— I never meant—"

Goldfarb looked from him to Maddox with horror, incredulity, an unwilling pity, dawning realization.

"Get up, Mr. Rhys," said Maddox. "Get into the car."

"Sergeant—"

"I'm sorry," said Maddox. "I'm sorry." He thought that Benjamin Goldfarb's expression would haunt him for years to come: the irrevocable, total tragedy in Goldfarb's eyes.

They got Rhys into the car. He was sobbing convulsively.

"My God," said D'Arcy. "My God. This—"

"I keep thinking," said Maddox, "of a thing Mrs. Rasmussen said. You can't expect children to be—anything but children. You know, D'Arcy, you can't expect people to be anything but people. Equipped with human nature. And they do sure as hell come all sorts."

In silence, they got into the Frazer-Nash. In silence, they started back for Wilcox Street.